JANITORS

OF THE LATE SPACE AGE

Satoshi Karasu

Editor: Draško Roganović

Cover art and illustrations: Darko Perović

ISBN: 9781521516218

Prologue

The first human to set foot on another planet was a fourteen years old North Korean girl named Bong-Cha. She spent seven long months starving and sweating in a tiny capsule, before safely landing on Mars. Then she broadcasted her momentous message calling for all people to unite under a common ideology. She died one week later.

For decades, her isolated country was secretly improving its space program under the pretense of developing nuclear weapons. Posthumously, they awarded her with the 'Hero of the Democratic People's Republic of Korea' medal, and erected a solemn bronze statue in her birthplace. As with other pioneers of space exploration, Bong-Cha's journey was only made public after its success. Her message from Mars achieved its purpose and united the people behind a common goal, adding wind to the sails of the stumbling space industry.

But it would take another broadcast, much, much later, to truly usher in a new era of space exploration.

First segment: The Late Space Age

When asked about his progress, the third (and last) governor of Mars famously replied:

"This planet laughs at our efforts to transform it into yet another Earth."

1.   Chinamen of Mars

A peaceful jazz tune was playing in the background, but when he opened his eyes the reality didn't match the mood. He pondered if he should simply close them again. That would solve the problem of an all-encompassing honey-toned planet seen ominously approaching through a cracked cockpit. There was a sticky lump in his mouth. With disgust, Sev realized it must be his own blood, but spitting it out now would create a mess inside the helmet, so he forced himself to swallow. Gross. Displays around him were blinking with a multitude of warning symbols. With a limp hand he decreased the volume of the jazz tune and pulled on the navigator hood over the helmet, the enhanced head-up display bringing those same warnings, but as a more subtle row of icons showing inoperable damage and destroyed modules.

"Ship: get me out of here," he muttered, hoping that voice commands are still operational.

"Negative. Not enough fuel for safe landing."

"Calculate all possible trajectories. Can I use what fuel I have left to get into any kind of stable orbit?"

"Negative. Not enough fuel for the maneuver."

Shiny pathways were displayed on his HUD, every single one ending in a projected crash over the bleak surface below. Computers were good at calculating these things. There will be no tricking the tried and tested laws of physics, no escape, no denying the irresistible pull of Mars. He was going down, and his ship – or what was left of it – was just a metal coffin, with not enough juice left to get away or safely land. Judging from the distance, they were still in the Clutter belt, and about to enter a ring of lower density where Phobos cleared some of the junk away.

"Calculate using Phobos moon for orbital slingshot maneuver. Give me anything! I just need more time."

"Negative. Phobos moon is out of reach."

"Why are you being so negative?" Sev sighed.

He had no recollection how he got here. His mind was numb, and a sinister sense of calm was taking over. That was Mars, though. He was sure of it. Like so many others, the red planet tricked him, and all the shadows of its craters resembled tiny, mocking smiles.

Only a few days ago, he was safely riding his rover between those craters, down on the surface...

***

When he was a kid, Sev dreamed of being an explorer in a high-tech rover on a distant planet. Now all the pieces were here. His view through a thick reinforced window opened up on a calm Mars vista. In the morning like this, a deep contrast of firebrick brown and orange red would sit like a crown on the peaks of dead, barren craters, but come noon the sand would turn an uninteresting hue of yellow or even a timid, pale brown, depending on the area he was currently in. And the nights, after an anemic sunset, were just pitch black with two tiny moons reflecting little light.

Slurping an orange-flavored puree to a calm melody of Tuvan throat singers, he was absorbing a splendid sunrise in his cockpit when an unidentified contact warning flashed on the head-up display. The radar blip approached lazily from the southeast and seemed to cause no harm thus far, apart from interrupting his peaceful morning routine.

"Chinamen!" he said with a disdainful smirk, tracking the bright dot on the radar display.

Mars was void of true Martians, except for a few shriveling blotches of adapted lichen - a failed experiment smuggled in by rogue terraformers during the golden age of Martian colonization. Like everything else, the colonization failed miserably, leaving behind a wild bunch of prospectors, miners, escapists, exiles, writers, adventurers, pacifists, conquerors, missionaries, tourists, scientists, "scientists", hermits and robots. So much wasted talent. For no particular reason, Sev used a blanket-term *"Chinamen"* for all of them. Many have already abandoned the red planet, deeply disappointed with what they've found, leaving their junk, dilapidated colonies and various automations behind. Forgotten robots couldn't die, so they pressed on with their menial tasks until a veil of dull red dust covered their solar panels, temporarily shutting them down. Then sometimes at night a storm would pass through a valley, and with the first rays of morning light a bunch of wind-cleaned robots would hobble about as if resurrected, thoroughly confused: *"Where has everybody gone?"*

A bizarre thing happened on Mars, leaving it semi-deserted. It wasn't some global disaster, rather a sort of saturation after an initial boom. A very human *"been there, done that"* mentality led to a sudden drop of interest for the whole space industry. A similar hiatus already occurred at the beginning of the space age; the same moment humans set foot on the Moon marked the end of the first Space Race and paved the way for decades of stagnation. Carved up and commodified by entrepreneurs, Mars turned out to be just another overhyped novelty, a meaningless conquest made for short-term gains.

It burnt up so bright, and so fast.

The blip crept at constant speed in a straight line, so Sev concluded that it must be a wandering drone. Those could be volatile, and he had no intention of crossing paths with it, or with any of the other weirdos this planet had to offer these days, whether robotic or fully sentient.

Grudgingly, he finished his breakfast and tossed the aluminum package into an automated cargo compartment for later recycling.

The volume of throat singing was temporarily lowered to accommodate an annoying audio warning: *"Unknown contact approaching!"* Unalarmed, he lowered his legs from the control panel and punched the ignition button, spreading pleasant vibrations throughout the cockpit as the electric engine buzzed to life. He gently increased the throttle and the nineteen-ton rover started to crawl to the top of a grey dune and out of the shadow, its matte ocher armor plates absorbing the weak morning sun. The semi-automated vehicle quickly adjusted its suspension, steering and even tire pressure for the desert terrain ahead and, under Sev's command, accelerated to a cruising speed. On the head-up display the blip made no suspicious movements and was slowly left behind as the *Master Control* rover gradually increased the distance, dancing over the lilac dunes.

Riding in MC was a joy. Even though the steering was massively assisted, that good feeling of *being in control* of something powerful was still there, and the sense of confidence and safety in this armored monster wasn't hindered by the fact that it was free of armaments. The only turret hardpoint on this modular vehicle was occupied by a laser antenna dome, an expensive long distance communication device that could reach Apex Corporation communication satellite in orbit. Sev wasn't worried about the lack of weapons onboard, his mission was to avoid danger and MC could, despite its weight, outrun anything that was out there. He just had to play hide and seek, and the broken topography of Mars was a perfect playground for it.

His next dropzone was in the Tharsis region. Once he gets out of the dune sea the rest of the trip will be flat and boring, but perhaps he'll be able to achieve high speeds, or maybe even set a new personal speed record – the fastest man on Mars! He wondered if he might achieve that title, now that the safety precautions were left in the hands of bored engineers such as him.

"Unknown contact approaching!" came another automated warning, delivered by a slightly disinterested female voice. There were no indicators on the HUD that...

The whole vehicle shook from a sudden impact that almost flipped the massive rover. Deaf from the explosion, Sev fumbled for controls inside the shaking cockpit: a web of cracks spreading over the side window. The interior was already filling up with smoke and smell of burnt plastic.

"Warning! Projectiles incoming! Execute evasive actions!" the automated warning is delivered, a bit too late.

"You will hold!" Sev ordered his machine and jerked the control wheel to the side, deft turn lifting billows of brown dust. The attack occurred with MC cruising at high speed, and judging by the fact that he was still in one piece, he could safely say it was a miss – but a near miss nonetheless. It became clear to him that the 'unknown contact' was actually a territorial drone of some kind, eager to pursue and destroy any trespassers.

"Warning! Projectiles incoming! Execute evasive actions!" came another warning, but this time Sev was able to steer his rover under a nearby dune just in time to hear and feel an explosion completely obliterate his cover. Pink sand and rocks were falling all over the place, stirring up a thick cloud of dust that obscured his vision. Modern targeting systems wouldn't be fooled by this primitive silicate jamming, but all he could do now was to increase the throttle and hope that the sensors will warn him of any obstacles ahead.

"Chinamen drone!" he yelled again, shell-shocked and angry.

Within seconds the rover was out of the dust cloud, multiple orange pathways now opening up between the dunes ahead. Sev thought about laying low but quickly realized that this would limit his speed, and all he wanted was to get out of here as soon as possible.

"Warning! Proj..." he switched off the annoying warning system, and resolutely flipped a small red switch on the overhead control panel, labeled *"Thruster"*. Modular construction allowed land-based vehicles and spacecrafts to share the same components, and this MC rover was unorthodoxly fitted with a small hydrogen thruster installed to assist the climb over steep slopes. It was supposed to be fired cautiously – and only in short bursts – but Sev barely thought about safety as he stepped hard on the gas paddle, machine growling approvingly as it ate through a tiny supply of hydrogen stored as a byproduct of oxygen-generation process. The acceleration kick was immense; Sev felt his head sink deep into the headrest just as another explosion went off behind him. The audio warning system would've had something to say about an obstacle dead ahead, but luckily it was turned off. The lower gravity on Mars made the rover feel deceptively light, but a head-on collision would wreck it nonetheless. At speeds like these the steering wheel would lock, so he could do little else but brace for impact as a menacing wall of sand appeared straight ahead. Luckily, the automated suspension system lifted the fore section, absorbing most of the shock and sending them up and over the summit, flying through the air on a cascading bridge of sand.

Mid-air, in an armored rover definitely not built for flight, Sev actually smiled! It was a deranged, twitching smile, but it was there. He broke his own speed record then and there, but then a painful landing quickly sobered him up. He was shaken, but still in one piece. The thruster was dry and the MC has taken a serious hit to the flank. Now they were in an open, flat area where they could really outrun anything. Adrenaline rush was finally catching up with him, bringing the shakes to his fingers and the chill of cold sweat on his nape. Sev set his sight on the shimmering horizon and pushed the throttle lever forward.

Like the dust-storms of Mars, the MC rolled over vermillion plains and out of harm's way.

***

Two hours later, he was still clutching the wheel and cruising at top speed over pristine dust plains, the massive wheels raising a murky cloud behind him. He wasn't feeling too good, and as adrenaline subsided, a strange anxiety settled in. With a shaky hand he finally pulled the throttle lever and the good machine complied, obediently slowing to a halt with the cloud of dust slowly catching up and shrouding it. He turned the engine off and finally there was some silence. For a few minutes Sev rested his head on the wheel, breathing and thinking about nothing at all.

"Damn retarded Chinamen, almost got me this time." he vented off some anger, maybe even fear.

With each month, it was getting harder to justify what the hell he was doing here.

Inhaling deeply, he braved to look around the rover in an attempt to assess the damage, but couldn't see anything wrong apart from the cracked glass itself, and some wispy smoke rising from the rear. If he was to attempt repairs, he would have to do it from the outside. There was a door at the back of his cockpit, but it led nowhere. He could turn around in his flight seat, comfortably stand up next to the door, slide it open into the wall section and there would be no way out – only the corrugated panel of cargo module blocking the doorframe. He had the prefabricated modular construction to thank for the door-to-nowhere.

His smartsuit hissed, sealing him in the moment he lowered the golden visor into position, and it only took a second more for the airlock system to suck out every last breath of oxygen from an entire cabin, as the massive bulletproof glass hemisphere above him was lifted by powerful motors. He was slightly worried that the explosions warped the geometry of the whole cockpit, but he could hear no strange creaks as it rose steadily, revealing a calm, straw-colored plain.

He was standing in a nineteen tons of good engineering. Dual cockpit design housed in a rugged – yet highly mobile – ocher-colored chassis came from a different time, when it was imperative to keep the precious crew safe. Powerful and unrelenting, this relic of the past was the perfect embodiment of that ancient human ambition to tame the red planet. But those ambitions were extinguished long ago...

"Alright, let's see how badly they've hurt you, eh?" he said, as if sympathizing with his ride. "And hey, at least we broke that speed record, didn't we?"

The machine didn't reply.

Coarse yellow dust screeched like snow underfoot, as he walked around the protruding forward wheel suspension, feeling the ridges of the bent armor plating with his palm. MC was an extension of his body, keeping him alive and mobile on this dull planet; it was his shelter, his lungs – and every dent in the armor made his skin crawl, as if he was stroking a nasty scar on his own skin. *There!* The point of impact was a nasty, star-shaped burn mark, but the projectile seems to have been deflected by the slated armor and exploded just above the vehicle, melting the upper sheets of dorsal carapace.

Stripped of any means of production, Mars was a junkyard and finding replacement parts was always a challenge. When he was a kid, he dreamed of being an explorer in a high-tech vehicle on a distant planet. Now everything he dreamed of was here, yet somehow flawed, as if he had made a deal with some twisted higher power.

He let out a tired sigh and prepared the tools for field repairs.

2. The Space Cavemen

"This is your first excursion from the *Mommy* asteroid, yes?"

"Yes," I replied.

"Don't worry," beak-nosed Laszlo assured me, a mischievous grin visible through his visor. "You're in good hands."

I remained silent. He and the other two members of the tribe were probing for a sign of weakness, and sooner or later they will pry something tasty out.

"Brothers, it seems they've sent us a dud this time," the mistress of the tribe sneered, a green-eyed girl barely a year older than me, who introduced herself as Kali. "How old are you, *kid?*"

"I'm five."

"Five!? Don't you give me that Ceres haughty talk, *kid.* You are floatin' with us now, far, far away from Mother Asteroid, so you better make sure we speak the same language. Let's try again, 'cause I really like you an' your new, milky white skinsuit. Mmmm, I bet it smells nice and fresh inside, doesn't it? Now, how old did you say you are?"

"I'm... around 15." It's easy to calculate how old I would be if I was born on Earth and, judging by her mangled vocabulary – which she probably picked up eavesdropping on stray signals coming from Earth –I'm guessing that's the kind of answer she is looking for.

"Oh, now you're talkin' dirty to me! We have a Terran mole among us, brothers! Aleeeerrrrt! All the way from rotten Earth!" They had me now. Let the feast begin.

Scrawny Alber, the third boy, joined in with fake politeness in his voice: "So, how is our grandmother these days?"

"I don't know, never been there." I replied, avoiding his eye.

"Forget it!" Kali's commanding voice prevented the approaching shower of taunts. "The toddler ain't worth the effort we are giving him. Listen up, milky boy: we know there's nickel ore on that asteroid above, so there's probably some platinum as well. Now, be a good boy and sniff it out for us, will ya? Consider it your initiation rite."

She threw herself at me and grabbed me by the ankle, using the momentum to hurl me toward the looming asteroid above, its presence revealed only via the absence of shiny stars, resembling a huge indigo lake. There's not much I can do about it, so I fall headlong into it, leaving them and our miner bathyscaphe spaceship behind.

"Let us know when you hit the ground!"Kali's cheerful voice ringed on my headset.

Sensation of movement is lacking, but I noticed the dark contour ominously swell around me as I approached, until I finally saw the flashlight's beam as a bright, expanding dot on the rocky surface. It helped me estimate the velocity and adjust my descent. *I can do this...*

Spreading my arms, I placed a signal for my suit to slow down. Slim as they are, Ceran skinsuits are driven by body motions and voice commands, like a regular spacecraft. *Am I still going too fast?*

"You're gonna squash yourself on your first descent, milky boy," one of the guys *encouraged* me, obviously watching from afar. "We'll send you back to Ceres as a frozen corpse."

I tried to pay them no mind, and with the bright dot expanding rapidly over misshapen asteroid surface I bent my knees to break the fall, lifting my elbows so the suit could increase the retro thrust. Without much of a fuss I landed softly on a polished rocky surface. *Phew, that went better than expected!*

"BOOM!" I heard laughter through the headset.

I think they like me, in a harsh, primitive manner.

There was no reason for me to cling to the surface, so I jumped and stabilized myself at some distance above, to better survey my surrounding. The surface looked molten and dull everywhere I flashed my light, so I turned on the ore detection sensor in my backpack for assistance. This brought up a luminous green, Lidar-generated topography overlay to my visor, revealing a cave – or, more likely, a mining shaft – not far away from my current position.

"Guys? This asteroid has already been prospected. There's a mining shaft here, did you know that?"

No reply from the jokers above, although I was sure they could hear me. With a hand gesture I transferred the green overlay to the corner of my visor and adjusted the flashlight for a closer inspection. It was definitely a mining shaft created by a standard, ship-sized rotating triple drill, its crude bite marks clearly visible on ribbed walls. I cautiously peeked inside, but the light didn't penetrate deep through dust and shoals of floating rocks, which must be a leftover from the crude dig. A Lidar scan, however, immediately revealed a wireframe of the entire 50-meters-deep tunnel, piercing the crust and branching into multiple smaller, hand-drilled passageways.

"Why are we exploring an asteroid that has already been mined in the past?" I wondered out loud as I leaned over the dust filled hole.

It made no sense why someone would go through all the effort of penetrating deep into an asteroid only to leave anything useful behind, and yet – this would be a perfect access point for my deep scan of the core.

"I am going down for a deep scan, guys," I said. And then, after an awkward pause: "And I know you can hear me. You are not scaring anyone!"

Out of habit I patted my helmet to check if it's there, and then pulled myself into the wide mouth of the mine, slowly floating deeper as if being sucked in by an unknown current. During my descent I broke apart delicate rock formations held together by microgravity. Best to keep my hands close, with those jagged walls all around. Ore scanner indicated the presence of nickel to my left, so I advanced cautiously into a narrow, hand drilled tunnel. The walls felt very close now, but they were chipped away with a different kind of drill and there was no fear of ripping my suit over a sharp protruding rock, so I used my hands and feet to crawl deeper inside. After a while, the tunnel suddenly expanded into what appeared to be an artificially made chamber.

"Oh... it's beautiful!" I said, almost out of breath. "You guys should definitely see this!"

The flashlight illuminated an unusually wide cavern, expanded from an existing crevice of some sort, with amazing, luminescent primitive paintings adorning the walls! Green glove prints left by some space cavemen could be seen in all directions, forming a beautiful fluorescent mural around the centerpiece – a circle representing a planetoid with torus-shaped base, surrounded by human stick figures, spaceships and drones. *That has to be Ceres, my home!*

Everywhere I point my flashlight that green paint burned bright, and I feel as if I'm floating in a forgotten shrine; a magnificent, vibrant sanctuary hidden inside a barren rock drifting through the void!

Lidar scan revealed this sacred cavern to be some sort of central hub in what must have been a sprawling nickel mine, with tunnels branching off in multiple directions. As I searched around with my flashlight, tracing those beautiful murals, abandoned bits of mining equipment came into view. A used drill rod. A broken lamp. A... whole skinsuit?!

It was floating perfectly still near one of the tunnels, awkwardly facing the wall, irradiated by the magical green cavern. I think I had a dream like this recently, and suddenly I felt very strange... I've heard bizarre rumors about exploited asteroids being used as tombs for my people.

And then, *something* that made its home inside that suit squirmed, producing a twitching motion in one of the sleeves.

A chilling tremor rose inside of me and I couldn't help but squeal in shock, my mind refusing to cope with the scene, when I heard a storm of laughter coming through the headset. The "empty" suit turned to face me and, of course – it was Kali, now pretending to claw at me like some kind of space zombie, while the group intercom was buzzing with laughter from the rest of my small tribe. Damn it! *I knew* I was about to go through some sort of initiation prank and still I felt stupid now that I fell for it. Hopefully this was the end of it.

"Oh, did you crap in your suit? It doesn't smell so nice anymore, does it?" Laszlo giggled and, moments later, appeared from one of the lower tunnels.

"You are watching too many of those pirated movies, Kali," I blurted out, still panting in shock.

"Like there's anything else to watch or do around here? Better get used to it. The Belt gets boring. All the fun we have comes from captured Earth signals and pirated entertainment, so you oughta cherish all the free thrills thrown your way."

"Well... Thank you," I muttered after a few seconds, and I meant it.

Joined by Alber, the whole tribe was cackling once more, getting high from all the green illumination in the sacred cavern.

"What is this place, Kali?"

"Dunno. Some of the miners must've been bored or high an' decorated the walls way before any of us were born. 'twas probably some of our ancestors, the first mad Cerans to hike through the Belt, painting their prophecies and ramblings caused by decompression sickness and oxygen-saturated diet."

"But how did you find this?"

"Same way you did. We were looking for a fresh platinum lode and stumbled into this green haven. S'nice, right? It almost feels warmer here just cuz of all the light."

"Guys, I have an idea!" Alber cried out, excited. "Let's leave our mark in the cave! We deserve it! I have a working industrial sprayer here!"

Agreeing instantly, we placed our gloved palms on the wall above, forming a four pointed star. Kali fumbled for something 'sacred' to say and, as if trying to buy some time, she asked me: "You didn't tell us your name?"

"I am Iyor," I said, relieved.

"Iyor? What kind of name is that?" Laszlo said, amused.

"I was told that it means *the Moon* in some dead language from Africa."

"Ha! I told you he's a Terran spy!" Alber barked, but the sting is gone from his voice.

"Listen up, boys!" Kali looked at each of us, obviously coming up with something appropriate to say. "This mural above us, this piece of art, and this story... it wasn't complete when the miners who painted it left. Their story is preserved to be cherished, and sometimes we can add our own little part, like we are doing right now. But the *story*... it's never complete - and it will never end!"

And with that she brought the muzzle over, blasting green iridescent industrial paint that immediately freezes and solidifies over our extended hands and as we lift our palms a strange imprint resembling a twenty fingered star is revealed on the wall of the ancients. Its ominous shape seemed slightly out of place – at least for now.

3. Clang!

From her spacious cockpit, she saw the Sun tearing through the infinite darkness every four seconds. Due to rotation of the craft, her cabin alternated between blindingly bright and pitch black. It felt as if she was taking part in some long-obsolete astronaut endurance test, a mild nausea building at the base of her tongue.

There are no dorsal or ventral thrusters installed on her cargo spaceship, the *Narwhal,* so the annoying rotation took place during the acceleration procedure, so as to keep the ship on course. A slow roll allowed two lateral engines to compensate for the obvious design flaw and correct the trajectory if needed. However, the drawback was that it also made it impossible to keep the solar panels aligned toward the Sun at all times. As a pilot, Anokha actually spent most of her time managing the fragile balance of power on the family cargo ship. To help her get a hold of herself during the grueling acceleration, she would sometimes sing, or summon a snippet of Zen wisdom. Usually it helped.

"I feel dizzy." she said with a tortured voice.

"You have less than ten minutes before dropping out of communication range, and you're already acting all space-bitten and weird." - Lero's haughty voice came over the speakerphone.

"Sorry, I... It's hard to get used to this constant spinning. It's driving me mad. After a full hour of acceleration I can get back to normal, but then I'll have to get used to the *lack* of it. Bah..."

"An hour? Oh right, your ship is fitted with that meager ion thruster."

"Why do you think they handed this supply contract to the Jágr family? It's certainly not because we are the fastest contractor – it's because we pitched the lowest offer. And we pitched the lowest offer because we fly this piece of trash that... Can we talk about something else, please?"

"Sure. Umm... When will we have the pleasure of seeing you again, Anokha?"

"When the stars are right, Lero! Seriously, it's going to be a long time before Earth, Mars and you are in such a... lucrative alignment."

Narwhal and the much larger, tuning-fork-shaped *F.S.S. Vladivostok* have just separated after being docked together for two standard days. Slowly increasing the distance, Narwhal was now blasting back toward the core of the Solar System.

"What does the *F.S.S.* stands for, anyway?" Anokha inquired.

"It stands for *Fringe Science Station*. We conduct trials and procedures that would take years to approve inside any legal system, so people just send us snippets of research data to quickly confirm them before they proceed with an expensive and long experiment."

"Can't you do the same thing on the Moon or somewhere closer? And I don't think... I don't think you can simply dodge regulations by moving..."

"Nobody here cares what you or anybody else thinks, Anokha–that is the whole point! We are unshackled from all conventions. Look, it's fairly simple: you send us a prototype for a test run or data to verify, and the only laws that we are bound to here are the laws of nature!"

"I still don't think that it's..." Anokha grumbled to herself.

"No, it makes perfect sense. You just can't think straight with all that spinning."

"Yeah... I guess you are right.

"So, what's your next stop?"

"Um, I am heading to Mars next, to pick up three containers and then back to Earth, my three month shift on this floating piece of trash is almost done." She was lying, but not much: a short smuggling detour to the Asteroid belt was also required, if this journey was to be profitable for her family.

"Mars? You must have a..."

And with that, the data link between them was no more.

"Hello?" Anokha muttered, checking the distance counter. "Well, that's strange."

And whenever you are forced to use the word 'strange' in open space you know something inexplicably dangerous is happening. They should be in range for dynamic short-distance communication for at least two more minutes, but apparently something went wrong. She fiddled with the settings to test if they are responsive, briefly managed to catch a glimpse of Lero's voice, distorted and multiplied and then – nothing.

There was no need to force their idle chatter over long-range communication. In fact, you never know who you'll attract with a stray long distance signal in this unregulated expanse, where even a distress beacon could bring more trouble than salvation. There were confirmed rumors of roaming pirate drones disabling lone traders in this area. Interchangeable modular construction made it notoriously easy for marauders and outlaws to grind your ship down for useful components and leave its husk floating like a ghost, to scare future generations. This place without laws that the science vessel enjoyed was just that.

Anokha sighed and tried to relax for the boring journey ahead. Space travel required a special state of mind, something she never fully mastered. To get her through, she glanced at the small, worn out photograph clipped to the control console. The picture was full of smiling faces. The Jágr family reunion. She smiled back.

Adjusting the bulky shutters on all sides to keep the maddening lightshow at bay, she squirmed in her flight seat, as if bathing in surreal darkness.

She was alone. All kinds of ticking, knocking, buzzing and humming sounds generated in the mechanical bowels of Narwhal were vibrating through the structure. *Tick. Knock. Buzz. Hum.* She yawned and lazily confirmed the autopilot coordinates are set for *Habakkuk* platform in the asteroid belt. The ion thruster was supposed to gently accelerate for at least another hour, that constant thrust pleasantly gluing her to the seat. *Tick. Knock. Buzz. Hum.* The door at the back of her cockpit module led to a small cabin with a sleeping chamber, but it was currently used to store extra food rations, so Anokha simply closed her eyes, falling asleep right there in her pilot seat, under a plethora of illuminated buttons and switches, but dreams eluded her.

Tick. Knock. Buzz. Hum. –Narwhal said at regular intervals.

Tick. Knock. Buzz. Hum.

Tick. Knock. Buzz. Hum.

Tick. Knock. Buzz. Hum.

Tick. Knock. Buzz. Hum.

Tick. Knock. Buzz. Hum.

Tick. Knock. Buzz. Hum.

Tick. Knock. Buzz. Hum.

Tick. Knock. Buzz. Hum.

Tick. **Clang!** *Tick. Hum.*

Upon hearing a subtle disharmony of her cockpit music, Anokha slowly opened her eyes. It should have been a *Knock,* but instead she heard a *Clang.* What's worse, there was no Buzz after that – just another *Tick.* She was intimately familiar with all the sounds of her ship and this *Clang* dude was not among them. Something, somewhere... was off. She waited for a few seconds in total silence, expecting the rogue noise to sound off again.

Oxygen generator, conveyor belts, assembler unit, thruster... all those modules generate some kind of sound at regular intervals, and she adopted all of them like close friends. A rogue sound could be a sign of a malfunction on one of the modules, some of which are vital for her life support. More than half way through the acceleration procedure, she faced a tough decision to either stop now, wasting a tremendous amount of power, or to attempt repairs once optimum speed has been reached. If she chose the latter, both she and Narwhal would be drifting through open space at terrifying speed, but relative to each other they would be standing perfectly still. She would need all her Zen gimmicks to stay focused at that moment.

Tick. **CLANG!** *Tick. Hum.* – said Narwhal.

There it is again!

Initiating the deceleration procedure now would turn Narwhal around and fire that same ion thruster in the opposite direction. More importantly, it would mean waiting for the battery to recharge again for a complete acceleration/deceleration cycle, as well as being late for her rendezvous in the asteroid belt. She wasn't really sure how the feral miners would react to a change of plans. The whole meeting was technically a smuggling operation, since they were under a trade embargo enforced by multiple corporations of Earth.

The thought of having to explain to her family that she missed a lucrative trade deal just to "check out a strange sound" made her decision that much easier. She was going to do an external checkup as soon as Narwhal hits cruising velocity.

***

"Oh girl, do you know where you're coming from..."

Anokha placed her shaky hand on the red lever, humming her

mantra song...

"Hey! Nothing is as clear..."

Velocity countdown display painted the whole cabin orange...

"Imagine in your mind oasis, far and wide beyond our living..."

Optimum velocity reached, almost there...

"...sure enough I'm tired out trying to hang on..."

Thrust down to zero, activating gyro stabilization!

"...while this world is spiiiiiining!!!"

The mantra song didn't help at all. After an hour of gradual acceleration, that faint blue emission from the main thruster flickered once more and died out. Heavy gyro motors kicked in, struggling to slow the rotation of the massive spaceship, all the while providing a range of squeaking sounds, while up in the cockpit module Anokha was still trying to cope with the diminishing of both the centrifugal force and thrust-generated push. When all the stars simply stopped moving, she felt weightless and disoriented.

It was eerily quiet now, without that pleasant white noise provided by the thruster. She sealed in her space suit and initiated the exit procedure, depressurizing the cockpit and leaving through a window section, with distant stars observing her every move. Childishly, she glared back at them. *Which one of you is Earth? I can't even recognize you. You're too far away.*

Everything seemed so still, like a photograph printed on a fine glossy paper, and it didn't give any comfort that the only sound reaching her was her own heavy breathing. At cruising speed, both she and Narwhal were zooming through space, but all the stars were so far away that nothing gave any impression of movement. It was better not to think about it too much, she decided.

Outside the cockpit module, floating free yet stabilized by micro thrusters of her suit, it was time to define some points of reference. Narwhal's beige hull would be 'down' on this space walk.

No, actually let's make it front, she thought as she turned to face the ship. It was so easy to change the perspective in free space. Now she started to climb 'up' the construction of her massive hauler, searching for burn marks or loose module sections. Even though she was in the vacuum of space, she could still *hear* faint sound vibrations of machinery by holding tight to the structure, her suit and bones acting as a conductor. Somewhere, something was making that occasional *Clang* that she didn't like.

Every component on the Narwhal was connected to... well... everything else, as there was no underlying structure or outer shell. *Russian Modular* is fundamentally different concept from old monolithic, single-piece spacecrafts by allowing reconfiguration of modules to suit changing needs, making every single segment reusable. This idea initially came as a surprise in a world where designed obsolescence found its way into every aspect of engineering, but this timeless solution gradually arose as the dominant construction option throughout the Solar System. The genius of this design is that each component block was compatible with every other, and when connected properly they would provide an airtight structure, capable of conducting both power and data.

Narwhal was spindle-shaped with weight distributed around the axis; antenna, gyro and cockpit modules were placed in the fore section, along with life support and massive battery blocks. Thrusters and solar arrays were grouped in the aft, connected via a spine-like extension. Central section consisted of bulky cargo holds and a precious assembler unit for quick repairs. She found no sign of external damage anywhere on the surface.

Anokha pushed herself upward: "Where are you hiding, my little gremlin?"

Every segment came with a small control panel that allowed both local manual override and access to the entire network grid.

There was no central computer, as every spaceship was actually a hive of modules, each equipped with just enough of its own computing power, so that with each added segment the computing power grew, allowing for endless expansion or effortless downsizing. Damage was also easy to localize and repair. This was so much more advanced than expensive single-piece spaceships of old that came with a 'central nervous system', mimicking their creators.

Scrambling around the bone-colored hull all the way up to the quiet thruster nozzle, she thoroughly examined each component along the way. Then she rolled over to the oxygen generator, conveyor system and assembler unit: poking, listening, searching... For a moment she wondered if she was overthinking the whole thing; Narwhal was an old ship, and maybe this new sound was just her building character?

The ship started to rotate!

But why? Gripping the rail tightly to resist the sudden centrifugal push, she felt an onset of panic.

She would have to return to the cockpit to find the cause of this erratic behavior. But after a few seconds, the ship stopped turning. Anokha blinked, her confusion bordering on fear now.

Half turn? Why? But of course! The autopilot system was obviously engaged for whatever reason. The ship was turning for... oh no! She had to get back into the cockpit before the thruster fired up for deceleration.

Distancing herself away from the hull, Anokha pushed her shoulders to the back, smart suit interpreting the signal correctly and igniting multiple micro thrusters that allowed her to quickly fly down to the cockpit. The massive ship below her felt oddly still. She climbed into the cockpit, closing and sealing the window section behind her with some relief, and as the cabin slowly pressurized, her hands raced over the controls trying to find an explanation for this maneuver.

Good, their trajectory was not in jeopardy; Narwhal was still floating toward the miner's base in the asteroid belt. But the autopilot system took over for some reason, preparing for a planned deceleration maneuver with still days to spare. It was...

It was as if there was *no pilot* present on board the ship. In that scenario Narwhal would go through the waypoints previously set by the captain, and safely return home.

"Huh? No pilot on board? No pilot on board!"

What had triggered the missing pilot sequence? She has left the cockpit, that much is true, but the suit transmitter should have been in range to signal that she is nearby. Following this line of thought, she accessed her wrist computer to see if the suit's radio emitter was operational. Sometimes a solution to what seems like a complex problem can be quite trivial. To test it, Anokha established a fresh communication link to Narwhal.

"Testing, testing," her own voice could be heard from the cabin speakers, confirming the datalink was healthy and bidirectional. But to her horror – there came a *reply!*

She was supposed to be alone on the ship.

It first emerged in series of low confusing sounds she barely noticed, like a whisper with too much echo that grew louder and louder with each repetition, as if struggling to get an incomprehensible message across. She tried to disconnect, but the awful noise – now as loud as a scream– went on for a few more increasingly terrifying loops. Her ship was speaking to her.

4.   The glow in the night

Welding steel armor plates and occasionally doing a little dance in the Martian dust to the tune of *Mr. Cab Driver* was not how he wanted to spend the day, but Sev managed to make the best of it. On a junk world like this, you are forced to salvage everything – even your mood. But things sometimes get in the way.

"Well... this is bad." He just fished out a small bent actuator from an exposed internal structure.

It was a tiny, insignificant thing, this simple micro-motor component in his hand. Yet it suggested that the blast has pushed its way deeper than he thought, shaking the very understructure of the MC. And this particular actuator was part of the most complex module on the rover – the laser antenna dome. To maintain long distance communication with the company satellite, gizmos like these helped stabilize the antenna and keep it focused on a distant dot in the sky hundreds of kilometers away. Without the antenna he was effectively off the grid, and with the Sun already closing down on the horizon, bringing a waning blue tint to the sky, Sev decided to postpone repairs and continue his journey to the Tharsis region. Leaving the work half-done would lead to a disquieting ride: where would he find the components needed to fix the antenna?

He collected all the twisted scrap metal strewn around, and assembled the tools into a small cargo compartment in the back. After a crucial adjustment to the playlist on his wrist computer, he was ready for a high speed ride to the sounds of traditional Finnish death metal. He was a musical omnivore. A hog, really.

***

The damaged rover was out of vermillion flats just before nightfall, entering an area of mellow rocky hills. It was comfy and warm inside the insulated cockpit. A faint glow on one of the distant hillsides attracted his attention, and he mused if it was just a natural reflection from the blue sunset, but after watching it for a while he concluded that it must be artificial, and for a moment he even thought he saw some kind of a pointy, silo-like structure at the base of the hill.

"Could be a ruin," he muttered to himself. "Or Chinamen ambush."

Although he could continue with the 'dry' repairs on the crucial antenna module in an open desert, he liked the idea of actually working in some kind of shelter, so he switched the headlights on and steered the wounded MC toward the unknown source of light.

Radar confirmed that there is a single, peculiarly shaped structure ahead. No vehicles and no detectable automated defenses. As they got closer, he observed small red navigational lights on some kind of spire and, with the night slowly settling in, a tall industrial lamppost faintly illuminating the area. Reducing his speed to appear less menacing, he was carefully closing in, unsure if his approach was noticed. He also remembered to turn the irritating audio warning system back on, just in case things get heated.

Nothing.

He braved driving up to about a hundred meters, before coming to a full stop on top of a stout hill, in plain sight of the ruin. It was... it was a church? Small, white, modular habitat base with a central dome surrounded by four smaller ones. He could not make out the symbol on the dome yet, but he thought he saw a distant figure in a green spacesuit exiting the airlock module. Sev hesitated for a second, and then decided to do the same.

Now that he was standing in an open cockpit, clearly exposed, he brought up his low-light monocular, pressed it to the visor, scanned the strange church with its only apparent inhabitant and, like a mirror image, he saw the person in the green environmental suit stare right back at him through a binocular. Sev paused and then slowly lifted his hand in the intergalactic greeting gesture.

He waved.

He could see the other person wave back, though not too energetic. Good. They stood there, awkwardly eyeing each other through telescopes for a couple more seconds, and then the green suit beckoned him over. Sev gave a thumb up and dropped back into the cockpit, directing the rover toward the white church. Chance encounters like this one were not uncommon on Mars, and with all the abandoned ventures there was certainly room for them, but the automated defenses, loonies and territorial drones made everyone wary of strangers.

A lone, heavy-framed resident was waiting for him, wearing his battered green enviro-suit: an older model. There was no sign of any vehicle, not even tire tracks around the entrance. Weird. The church-outpost was large and in decent condition, albeit covered with a brownish patina. Sev looked on in silence as the green suit approached, slowly examining the vehicle. The night was setting in, only light coming from that tall pillar with a pair of industrial lamps.

Sev pushed the cockpit open and, still feeling somewhat protected, turned on the voice amplifier on his helmet. The sound was modulated by a specialized low frequency device to get through the thin Martian atmosphere.

"Hey there!" he said cheerfully. "I know it's getting late, but I was wondering if you have time to talk about our Lord and Savior?"

"It's never too late," a deep, mature male voice delivered the reply, and Sev couldn't be sure if he was serious or following up on the joke.

"I'm actually just looking for a place to finish some precision repairs, and then I'll be on my way. Can you provide me shelter? I am open to barter."

"You are welcome here. Please, come inside." And with that, the green suit turned around and headed toward the airlock module of the strange church.

Sev examined the small outpost again. There were no religious symbols, yet the layout reminded him of domed churches for some reason: shabby-looking, with worn out modules, sand-blasted by countless storms. A rust-colored dune already engulfed one of the domes. Eventually, Mars will swallow it whole. Now he could see that the domes were actually hydroponic farms, yet his initial impression about this being some kind of house of worship lingered on.

He jumped out, secured the MC and then ran to the entrance module, the large green man already waiting for him inside the airlock chamber. Now that he could see his face through the orange visor –the bushy grey beard and thick eyebrows on a sun-kissed face – he felt much better.

"You look like Santa Claus," Sev giggled.

"But that *is* my name. I am Klaus," he grinned pleasantly, various lights blinking inside the small chamber suddenly reminiscent of Christmas lights. "It's a pleasure to meet you."

"Nice to meet you too, Klaus. I'm Şevket, but just call me Sev. What kind of outpost is this?"

"It's a *Gurdwara*, I believe. A Sikh temple of sorts, where people from all faiths – as well as those that do not profess any faith – are welcome. I found it empty and moved in after I retired, three years ago."

A blast of air thoroughly cleaned them of salty Martian dust and then a green, ornate door on the other side of the cylindrical chamber rolls open, revealing a solemn hall of combined living modules with colorful carpets and tapestries. With the dense, pressurized air around them, Sev could hear a multitude of tiny noises, something he dearly missed when all he usually heard was the sound of his own breathing. He followed Klaus into the main hall that was bathed in warm colors, lights and... was that a faint smell of coffee in the air? Everything seemed worn out, but clean and well-maintained. There was even a bookshelf with actual paper books! In the center was a large table designed for at least eight people, but on it was only a single plastic tray, a sign of an interrupted dinner. Sev slowly took off his helmet and ran his fingers through his unkempt hair and beard, something he couldn't afford to do for a long time.

"I'm sorry I interrupted your dinner, Klaus."

"Please, no need for pleasantries. Make yourself at home, there is plenty of room. I only ask of you that you leave everything in good condition," he said in a choppy manner, with a hint of German accent.

Sev took a few steps around, admiring the interior, but stopped before actually stepping on the carpet. He should take off his suit first; moments like these are a real luxury on Mars. Klaus already hung his helmet near the airlock door and was in the process of peeling off his green space-suit, revealing a Brusska company logo on the back of his khaki coveralls.

"You used to work for Brusska? I guess that technically makes us colleagues, as I am prospecting for Apex."

"I'm retired," Klaus sighed indignantly. "The company went bankrupt years ago, its assets on Mars pulled apart by nouveau riche companies such as that Apex of yours. Isn't that how you got hold of the MC rover outside, hmmm?"

"There's no point in bringing any more of those heavy vehicles all the way from orbital factories of Earth. The cost must have been terrific! Apex just merged with the whole bunch of dead companies, and they sent me here on an automated capsule – it's cheaper for them that way!"

Now only in his insulated coveralls, Sev stepped on the deep soft rug with his bare feet and immediately felt like he was at home, although for him the very idea was an abstract one. It was a wool carpet. Wool from sheep, from Earth, transported all the way to another planet. That's crazy!

As he looked around at all the personal items scattered in this large room, it suddenly became apparent that Klaus was one of those "company assets" left behind, forgotten and stranded on Mars. Old, bald and plump, Klaus was bent over one of the cupboards, searching for a proper food ration for his guest, and seeing him like that, Sev realized that the tone he was using earlier could have hurt the retired man.

"Klaus, I'm sorry."

"Forget about it, Sev. If you're smart, you will realize that you are looking at the picture of yourself in a few years' time. The companies come and go, they merge, they lend you, they outsource you, and they do anything they can to make you feel as an insignificant part of "the big picture" – as if being alone in Space, the biggest thing there ever was and ever will be, isn't enough of a downer already. C'mon, let's drink some homemade Martian moonshine, and forget about the whole thing..."

Sev didn't drink alcohol, but he felt obliged to at least keep his host company.

***

Two hours later, even after giving it their best effort, they still couldn't forget about *the whole thing*, mumbling about their predicament.

"Maybe we just don't have it in us anymore," growled Klaus. "Mining is the only profitable venture left. There are abandoned theme parks on Moon, ghost colonies on Mars, and even churches like these, staring empty into the void from God-forsaken corners of the Solar system. I'm tellin' you, Sev – we are witnessing the end of the Space Age. A dead end! What we need now is some kind of new compound or material to facilitate a new era of human technological advancement; or a messiah; or just a master reset in the form of a big war. Just... *something* to get the blood flowing, lest we be finally forced to admit to ourselves that we are not meant to be a space-faring race. We lost it, somewhere along the way, and now we grew tired of searching! I'm sorry." Hiding his face behind wrinkled hands, he was probably crying.

Nodding approvingly, Sev tilted his glass, capturing a fleeting glint on the rim. Somewhat sleepy, he examined the beautiful, fragile speck of light before it slipped away.

5.   The maddening signal

She needed time to think, and, fortunately, time was all she had in this malfunctioning ship. Anokha narrowed down the problem to the main communication module, a long antenna array in the fore section that served as a detection, identification and communication instrument, but currently it was misbehaving like an autistic child with a megaphone. First it failed to detect the presence of the pilot near the ship, which triggered the autopilot procedure, and just moments ago it broadcasted this unspecified radio transmission, something like an S.O.S. beacon.

A strong signal released in the Outskirts area was like a game of Russian roulette – you feel lucky if *nothing* happens. She still had two days before the deceleration maneuver for her planned rendezvous and trade with the brutish miners of the asteroid belt. These Cerans, named after their central base on Ceres asteroid, were something of a modern mystery, and by the time she reaches their Habakkuk barter platform her antenna should be 100% operational, lest she be identified as a threat and shredded to bits by automated defense drones. Vague trade restrictions imposed by corporations of Earth hit them hard, supposedly making the savages all jumpy and on high alert for some fleet of mercenaries that could show up at any moment.

"I wonder if the guys at Vladivostok heard my S.O.S.?" Anokha said to herself. Their connection was abruptly cut short; another indication of a faulty antenna but... a strange and ugly idea started to take shape in some dark corner of her mind. She observed the silent stars, but they offered poor counsel, allowing her to contemplate and trace the events back to the moment the trouble started. It all pointed to Vladivostok, and that interrupted communication they've had.

She went through the entire comlog and found out that the connection was terminated due to a 'priority datalink', with a sudden spike in bandwidth and data being received on multiple frequencies. She was onto something here. Something was transmitted by the science vessel just moments before the line died out, and Narwhal's computers now struggled with the massive influx of stored data. Worse still, the amount seems to be... fluctuating, as if a complex, alternating encryption was constantly at work. She immediately attempted a data banks purge, but found it impossible to uproot this unwelcome guest.

"Those bastards!" Anokha yelled, honestly surprised. "They messed up my ship, saddling me with some kind of virus."

There was more evidence of corrupted data on the Narwhal, as some of the modules were unresponsive, claiming once again that some kind of priority process is underway. Carefully analyzing it, she found no indication of an elaborate scheme to take over her ship, it's just that everything responded sluggishly to her commands, and sometimes the results of her input would be swapped for something else, so the more she tried to fix things this way, the more tangled they became. Narwhal was a mess, suffering some sort of computational shock that made it revert to its autopilot in an attempt to bring the ship and its pilot to safety. There was no way around it: it was time for a hard reset.

There are ways to temporary 'kill' a ship in order to restart it, and with the computer reset unavailable, she could detach the main battery, or just slowly rotate the solar array and drain its power reserves. The problem, of course, was that she depended on the onboard life support so that she could continue with her journey. Still, she could survive a couple of hours only on her spacesuit life-support.

As she was planning the reset operation, a yellow warning light appeared on the radar. *Beep! Beep! Beep!* A new contact incoming, on an interception course. Anokha cursed, realizing that, whatever it was, it was probably attracted by that long range rogue S.O.S. signal she involuntary sent out.

It was a small, still unidentified vessel, and out here – no ID is bad ID. It could belong to a range of pirates, renegades and outcasts that made the hollow Outskirts their hunting grounds, and Narwhal was an unarmed hauler that couldn't outmaneuver or outrun a small craft. How did things slip out of control so fast? She was aware that a sense of control is an ephemeral thing, but for losing something so insubstantial, she felt an almost physical impact.

The contact above her abruptly changed course, and Anokha could see the counter presenting their distance gradually slow down to a standstill, meaning that they were now moving in perfect parallel trajectories. Flawlessly matching other vessel's speed was a clear indication of a drone. There were no attempts at contact. Nothing. Just two ships, flying in unison.

"Hello?" Anokha said with a frightened voice, attempting to reason with her silent escort.

Nothing. A quick scan of her stalker confirmed that it was a small, heavily armed pirate drone, an ugly but effective mash-up of different scavenged modules. Its current passive behavior was a mystery.

She felt powerless, even lost. The weight of the whole ship, now semi-responsive, came down upon her shoulders. What should've felt like a perfect extension of her body now burdened her like a thousand tons of dead steel, falling through space and dragging her by the umbilical cord of her life support system.

This moment of weakness will pass, and she wasn't just going to let things slide like this. She is a human being that can wrestle any danger thrown at her, and still come out on top. This is just a momentary loss of control. In time, she will figure it out, but for now, in this delicate moment of weakness, she just closed her eyes and fought the urge to break down and weep.

6.   Coffee from another planet

Sev woke up to the smell of roasted coffee. At first it just floated there, like a remnant of a dream, but it persisted even when he got out of the comfy bed. Looking around the small room, he could see an old calendar on the wall featuring that charismatic Korean cosmonaut-girl next to a 'Trust me – I'm an engineer' poster, some potted plants on a cupboard next to the bed, and a round window on the ceiling bringing in bright yellow mood to the room. It was late in the morning, but he didn't mind. He washed his face and stared at a stranger in the mirror. It will take more than a good night's sleep to bring back the face he knew. It was chilly inside the Sikh temple, so he slipped into his cleaned coveralls and walked over to the main hall.

"Was I blabbering too much last night, eh?" Klaus greeted him with a beaming face and two steaming mugs of coffee. Cheerful, and with that booming voice, he did remind him of Santa Claus.

"Nah, just something about crooked corporations trying to take control of the whole universe. It's what I expected to hear from a dismissed hermit like you. Now, is that really coffee? Where did you get that?"

"Aaaah, I wouldn't tell you even if I could remember."

They had a quiet breakfast, sharing different types of food rations and some fresh vegetables from the hydroponic farm, but coffee was the absolute star of their meal.

"I really appreciate that you've allowed me to stay here, Klaus. I feel thoroughly rested."

"You are welcome... colleague," Klaus chuckled. "Seen any good ore finds recently?"

"Oh no, they don't trust us with the raw data anymore. I only supervise a bunch of cheap rolling microbots that survey a large area, and transmit their findings directly via satellite back to Earth."

There was an awkward pause, interrupted only by munching and gulps.

"So, now you are just... what... a human liability? Then I should feel lucky to have worked during the golden age of prospecting. At least we needed to study Martian geology and analyze satellite readouts for promising land acquisition," Klaus exclaimed, his voice filled with bitterness.

"This *is* a follow up on your efforts, Klaus. They have narrowed it down, and now they use robots to pinpoint favorable areas. The only difference is that they don't bother me with the survey data. I keep the robots in good shape and transmit their findings up through the eye in the sky and I keep my mouth shut." Sev shrugged humbly. "Not really a glorious job, I know, and not at all what I imagined it to be."

"But then what's the point, Sev? Apex is prospecting, but they have no plans for actual manufacturing – they just want to acquire good cuts of land! I am sober now, and I will tell you again: Corporations have no long term plan for this planet, or anything outside of Earth! They have gradually removed all the production modules from Mars, to a point where we are left with just two refineries. Two refineries for the whole planet! And the few sorry souls we have left here are forced to mine and trade raw ore, if they want to get their hands on new components. We should revolt, if only they had some central authority here, but instead they just leave us to rot and eat each other. After years of hard work, I don't even have the means to go back to Earth – can you imagine that?"

"Oh, there's so much junk lying around, Klaus. I imagine an experienced engineer like you could easily assemble a little jet, we both know that." Sev munched slowly, eyeing the old man. "But you don't want to go back. Earth is a cesspool, and you know it."

"Yes," the old man's eyes gleamed with passion. "Overcrowded, stagnant... malign. Initial space exploration bubble spewed out millions of people to Mars, through the Belt and in the Outskirts beyond, so most of them perished or simply fell back to Earth, but you know what: some of them chose not to return– guys like you and me! We passed the natural selection process! We are meant for stars, unlike the slobs back on Earth, though they will never admit defeat and –like some dimwitted older brother –they'll always be there to keep us down, sapping our production on Mars and imposing this embargo nonsense on Cerans. Despicable!"

There was an unconstrained vigor in the old man, and he was obviously fond of making speeches, but they were passionate, unrehearsed and true, coming from deep personal experience rather than some established ideology. It was a lot to absorb, and Sev didn't understand half of it, but he could sense some kind of just anger behind it. He saw it for what it really was – a very human act of fighting stagnation. And inside of him, a seed of doubt was planted.

***

It took two days to complete the repairs to the MC. First they lifted the heavy, armored flank segment, exposing an automated cargo hold, oxygen/hydrogen generator and the dented foundation of the laser antenna module. It was delicate work, so Sev felt lucky to have an extra pair of hands and experienced advice from an old survivor. He was certain the old loner enjoyed some meaningful work as well.

"Listen, Sev, before you leave...I probably ended up venting some of my frustrations, and you had to keep up with my nagging every night. For what it's worth – I am sorry. I really enjoyed having a friendly face around here."

"I never interrupted you not because I was being polite, but..." Sev frowned, not used to directly saying what was on his mind. "I realized that your rage might be legitimate. Klaus, I am not just roaming the red planet anymore. From today on I will keep my eyes open and I'll be searching. For what – I am not sure yet, but I am not *content* with just looking at things as they are. That is all. I came to Mars because I wanted to make a difference and – seeing the rotten situation here – I thought it was the harsh environment that hindered any progress, but now I am starting to believe it's due to a terrible mismanagement. Which, it seems, I am a part of."

He nodded, and saw Klaus give him a strange, serious smile. The lower half of his bearded face smiled encouragingly but his eyes were afraid.

"Goodbye Sev, and good luck out there."

***

Zooming over mellow hills to the zany sounds of Synthwave electronic music, he tried to clear his mind. Nasty surprises this planet had to offer were still all around, but this glimmer of hope and positive energy he enjoyed in the dusty Martian Sikh temple made a lasting impact, and Sev felt stirred up.

He was two days behind on his planned journey to the Tharsis region, where he needed to secure the landing zone for an automated capsule delivering a dozen new prospecting microbots. He discovered that he was not looking forward to it at all. With the Apex satellite in proper position and the laser antenna repaired, he sent out his report and immediately received an urgent message waiting for him, probably for days now:

PRIORITY INSTRUCTIONS FROM APEX CORPORATION

CURRENT PROSPECTING MISSION SET TO LOW PRIORITY. NEW ORDERS: RECLAIM A STARCRAFT FROM BRUSSKA REFUELING BASE AND REPURPOSE IT FOR SPACE COMBAT. INTERCEPT AND HOLD THE INDEPENDENT MERCHANT VESSEL "NARWHAL" AND AWAIT ARRIVAL OF F.S.S. VLADIVOSTOK IN MARS SECTOR ALONG WITH FURTHER INSTRUCTIONS!

Intercept and hold? What does that even mean? Yesterday he was only a troubleshooter, Mr. Fixit, a glorified janitor of Mars, and now they tossed him into a role of a space pilot sent to 'intercept' a trader vessel. Being cut off for days, he wondered if he received the message too late.

7.   The repeating dream

With my feet entwined in the elastic net, I pushed the massive sheet of steel down into place.

"Click!" I said to myself, face sweaty from this backbreaking work.

Below me is the lean grey body of our unfinished miner bathyscaphe, wrapped in yellow construction net like a placenta. It's docked under the aquamarine lights of a spacious cylindrical construction platform, moored in place with multiple pipes and cables: an unborn ship in its mechanical womb.

It was easy to crawl over the bathyscaphe with a tow of heavy components, since no gravity was induced in the construction pen, but even so, my suit thrusters were starting to overheat. Piece by piece and module by module, a single space engineer could assemble and weld together a whole spaceship like it's some kind of toy. Complex components and instruments must be manufactured in an automated assembler unit, but robust blocks– like this armor coating– can be manually welded over. It's punishing work and, naturally, it's something *the new guy* gets saddled with.

I worked alone. Kali, Laszlo and Alber took our cargo bathyscaphe, laden with iron and nickel ore, to Habakkuk, an icy asteroid base not far away. Constructing a spacecraft without the assistance of robotic assembly arms is grueling work; even my skinsuit is 'tired' –its blinking yellow lights are begging me to recharge it. Although incomplete, our sarcophagus-shaped miner is already powered up with a chunk of refined uranium burning inside the reactor core, and as I grip the protruding recharge port, I could feel the connection with the unborn ship as power surged through my thirsty suit. A little bit of rest felt good. Through the gaps in the cylindrical construction pen, a multitude of stars were shining in like sapphires. Watching from inside, one would think of a serene night sky, but as soon as you went outside, the opposite would be true: open space is an endless, terrible day, with its one-eyed guardian constantly bombarding you with heat and radiation.

I tilted my head. *Oh, there it is again!* A reflection. And again. A small object... I could not quite judge the distance; but there was something there, rotating and reflecting the light in regular intervals. It couldn't be the rest of the tribe returning from Habakkuk, more likely a piece of debris, flying past at high speed. With the failed colonization of Mars – and partial colonization of the asteroid belt - there was always junk floating around, and sometimes you could even salvage something useful. But with our only operational bathyscaphe taken by the rest of the tribe, I could only watch as it zipped by, whatever it was.

No, wait... I could use the telescoping camera here in the construction pen! I pressed my visor to the rubber eyepiece and rotated the instrument, until the shimmering dot appeared in contrast to the blackness of space. At first I couldn't make out what it is, but as I focused the image a strange shape came into view – a space suit curled up in fetal position, rotating slowly!

Impossible! My mind raced for something to say, something to do, but I found myself simply overwhelmed at the improbability of it all. The floating body seemed so tiny and insignificant, so thoroughly swallowed up by the void surrounding it. It was paralyzing and depressing to watch, but there was nothing I could do about it.

Though, actually... I had a whole ship right here! The thrusters are operational, navigation equipment is installed, it was fully powered... it just lacked armor plating and some instruments, but with its strong propulsion I could easily intercept it. In theory at least. *The distance!* I checked the distance to the floating body. It was very far away, so the velocity at which it was drifting must've been amazing. If I was going to do this, I didn't have much time– I had to continue unhindered by overthinking.

Moments later, I was inside, closing the heavy lid above me. I've already disconnected all the cables and pipes that tied the ship inside its space womb. Nobody wanted its maiden voyage to be a rushed retrieval of what will surely turn out to be a corpse but.. *There I go overthinking again!* Power on. Inertial dampers off. Hydrogen thruster off. Ion engines on. I decided to use weaker ion thrusters for start. Throttle up! The sleeping whale has awoken, its body resonating with a soft buzz.

Still wrapped in the yellow construction net, the bathyscaphe is released into space, spiraling softly as it emerged from the cylindrical construction pen. In my haste I forgot to disconnect the oxygen coupler, and now it stretched and flailed around like an umbilical cord, dragging some of the scaffolding apart. Main thrusters on! The noise was real loud now, as hydrogen exploded behind me. I adjusted my course for the little bright dot I could barely see on the screen now. The cockpit of the bathyscaphe was buried deep inside the claustrophobic spacecraft, and since it had no windows, you had to navigate by heart and live camera feeds covering all directions.

The acceleration pushed me deep into the seat. With both hands on the control levers, I rolled the bathyscaphe on the boarding trajectory. There was no point for me to rush and intercept the drifting body; I could reach it faster but I could hardly avoid crashing into it at these speeds. Instead I had to get *behind* it and match its course. Only then I could increase my velocity and catch up to it. With both course and speed matched, it might be possible for me to get a hold of the drifting corpse. *Body! Not a corpse!* Why was I doing this? With the ship on course I allowed myself to actually think about what is going on.

A body drifting in space with no power signal coming from its suit? There's a 100% chance that its occupant is dead. Nothing can survive for long just drifting out in space; if the panic doesn't give you a heart attack, lack of oxygen or dwindling thermal protection will eventually end you. Space is the *anti-life*. There will never be any reconciliation with it. For generations we, the Cerans, believed we have gradually adapted to it, but you only needed to gaze into the endless void to know these efforts will never be enough to really call open space our home.

There it was. I could see it clearly on the main screen now. Straight ahead, a dead man in a Terran spacesuit. No sign of movement, no sign of life. An enigma. The body was revolving quietly, completing a small macabre pirouette every few seconds. The fact that it was a Terran suit meant that it was better left undisturbed, regardless of the reason it was drifting through Ceran space. And yet...

And yet, a strange feeling was coming over me, and it had nothing to do with curiosity. In Space, chaos reigns and coincidences are sacred. On Earth, they might call us savages, space primitives and worse, but we believe that coincidences are a manifestation of fate. Recently I observed *another* corpse in a space suit, floating in the sacred cave of our ancestors. Of course, it was only a prank the rest of the tribe played on me as an initiation rite, but the image was still clear in my mind. Was the cave of the ancients really prophetic, offering me a vision of things to come?

Speed matched. Whoa! We were moving at speeds of interplanetary travel. Course perfectly aligned. I tapped my helmet for good luck and pushed open the heavy lid, allowing to be pulled out by inertia. I drifted closer through space to the cream-colored spacesuit, curled up there like a baby. Exposed. Fragile. Calm. First sign of damage – an ugly burn mark snaking around its left forearm, where the wrist computer ought to be. Pensive seconds flow like hours, as we slowly drift closer. Finally, I gripped the ankle of the bulky suit. It was stiff. I pulled myself closer and observed my reflection in the mirrored visor. Carefully I pushed the protective golden layer up, revealing a delicate face of a girl, her locks of jet black hair glazed with sweat. She looked dead.

I was not scared. Dreams and fate have offered me glimpses of this moment, and now I felt oddly relaxed, as if calmed by the corpse.

There was a patch on her shoulder. It read: *Anokha Jágr–Narwhal*. Suit's integrity seemed intact, but the wrist computer had been... ripped off? There were clear grinder marks on the four corners, and the wiring had been forcefully slashed apart: a sign of madness perhaps? The body squirmed in my arms, but for some reason I was not surprised. My heart started to pound: not faster, but stronger. Without a wrist computer or power in her suit, I could not establish any sort of communication link, so I pressed my visor directly on hers and yelled hard, at the top of my lungs, hoping that the vibration will be transferred through her helmet.

"Hey! It's alright. I got you, Anokha. Anokha? Can you hear me?"

***

Anokha slowly opened her eyes. A stranger's visor was kissing her own, a muffled voice reached her ears, its vibrations waking her up from dreamless slumber. There was oxygen inside, but power and active thermal protection are gone, her suit only a hot stiff insulating cocoon around her.

"My name is Iyor. I'll get you out of here, OK?" the stranger yelled, his face still a blur.

Anokha blinked slowly, and attempted a smile.

8.   The vagrants of the Polar base

Rusty construction cranes and ramshackle towers of the Brusska refueling station were perched over the horizon, like huge dead birds overlooking an icy plateau. The polar base was built as a joint effort of multiple corporations to be the central hub for their mining operations on Mars. All of them went bankrupt long ago, their efforts seemingly wasted on the red planet. Nowadays, the area was inhabited only by terrifying winds, and they made their claim known by mercilessly pounding on anything that dared to stand tall on this frozen wasteland dotted with dark blotches of wild lichen. Wind-polished ice gleamed like amber in the morning sun, but the gloomy atmosphere turned it into dusk.

The armored rover tackled strong gusts of wind with ease as it made its way toward the ruins. Inside the cracked cockpit, Sev was feeling cranky from the sleepless night spent behind the wheel. Rare cirrus clouds could be seen above, but he found it hard to enjoy the show as those new orders from the company brought bitter realization about the nature of his job: he wasn't a brave explorer dedicating his life for mankind – he was just a corporate asset on a payroll, or at least that's increasingly how he felt. Drop everything, head south to Brusska refueling station, find an operational spacecraft, takeoff from Mars, meet with some kind of science vessel and "await further instructions". And just like that, he was pulled by an intangible string from another planet.

This was the furthest south he ever went. As he got closer, ice screeching under heavy wheels, Sev rose in his cockpit and tried to locate the main hangar with an old handheld monocular. Unfinished structures came into focus, dangling like scarecrows in the punishing wind. The base seemed small, but there must be more underneath the surface, safe from the elements. He located a landing platform beacon to his right and steered the rover there.

It was spooky, and not only because of the ice and the screaming wind. A windswept surface, with a tilted antenna tower and four large yellow squares marking the landing pad elevators, protected by a fin-like wind barrier. They'll be his way in. Sev parked his frosted rover on the closest elevator and waited.

Now what?

Dry wind was howling like a pack of predators, their territory invaded. A communication display blinked green, indicating some kind of automated transmission occurred and, with a rumble, the shaky elevator started to descend. The rover was recognized as its 'kin', originally belonging to the same bankrupt corporation. An airlock gate closed above him as soon as they descended below ice level, choking out the wind, as well as the only source of light along with it. Moments passed in darkness. The sounds were different now, indicating a large underground hangar of some sort. Here was his prize, here laid the spaceship that will take him to the stars, here was the...

With a low thump, the elevator suddenly stopped, and lines of bluish light immediately flickered to life illuminating an empty underground hangar.

There was *nothing* useful here. An expansive, triangle-faceted ceiling supported by massive red pillars formed a vast dome over a deserted, rusty hall, with elevator ramps and construction bays, but... they were all empty. And why *would* there be anything left? Everybody departed from Mars. The company has sent him here, without even bothering to check if he will find the means to accomplish his mission. It's like they didn't even care...

External pressure indicator was on, which meant the whole hangar was pressurized. This abundance of oxygen didn't come as a surprise – the base was intentionally located in the polar region, where automated drills dug below the dry ice layer searching for water ice to break it down into breathable oxygen and hydrogen fuel.

"What a bad dream," he muttered.

He selected the cheery *Masquerade Waltz* by Aram Khachaturian on his wrist computer, and then opened the cockpit, gently swaying to the rhythm. Directional spotlights from above provided a surreal, stage-like setting, so he picked up a mocking waltz trot, whisking over the elevator platform, with the ice brought down from above crunching underfoot. He danced his way down a short flight of stairs and lifted his visor, the cold dry air on his face immediately waking him up. There was something else there, beside the oily, workshop smell. He shone his spotlight on each of the empty construction cradles above. One contained a skeleton of a surface jet skimmer stripped down to its bare construction bones, hanging there like a corpse. He got carried away by the music, performing a little spin, and was shocked when a spacesuit-clad figure, interrupted in a prowling stance, came into view just a few steps behind him.

Sev instantly froze, eyes wide in disbelief. The figure seemed to be shaking nervously, clutching a long rusty crowbar, face obscured by a bulky helmet. Sev sheepishly raised his hand, and performed that intergalactic greeting sign.

"Umm... hello?"

"侵入者!" came an unexpected reply, as his stalker advanced with weapon raised, still shaking violently.

"Wait! Hold on! I didn't mean to..."

But the assailant didn't stop. Overhead crowbar slash fell heavy upon his shoulder, the semi-elastic rod ripping through his suit like a fishhook. The vicious swing was clearly aimed at his head, and though Sev managed to move it away just in time, the impact still pinned him down to the hard floor.

"Stop!" he cried out in pain, knowing all too well that the time for talking has passed, or had never even been there in the first place.

He needed room to get back on his feet, but the only 'weapon' he had was a flashlight, so he pointed it at his assailant's face. It was destroyed the moment he lifted it, pieces of plastic and glass exploding in his hand. He couldn't roll away, so he covered his head, bracing for another impact.

And sure enough, that steel rod slammed over his forearm like a slab of searing iron, pain flooding through his body. He started kicking, and managed to blindly hit at something, which provided him with some room for escape. Teeth clenched in pain, he rolled over his numb shoulder and finally used the momentum to stand up, his attacker but a pillar of stark shadows before him.

"Ok, ok... you play – you pay." Sev spit through his teeth and tauntingly stepped forward.

He was immediately met with a shower of brutal swings, but he sidestepped out of harm's way. Legs served him well, but his upper body hurt more with each raspy breath. He kicked at his enemy every time a chance presented itself. There was a method behind his movement: a fighting style developed a long time ago, used only to disrupt an opponent's stance. It laid in obscurity for decades, and people even forgot its name, until Zero G combat became a reality. Without solid footing, most established fighting concepts melted away, and found it hard to put any mass behind blows. This is when that ugly, patchwork, dance-like martial art made a comeback, and really benefited the initiated.

A savage swing whizzed past his ear, as Sev ducked away and planted a knee on his opponent's exposed hip. This put them both off balance in the deceptive gravity of Mars. His enemy instinctively reached out to grab him for support, and that's when Sev grappled his arm. They both crashed down on the cold grated floor. Sev held onto his opponents forearm and threw his legs around him for a better grip. Arching his back, he pulled with all his might, ignoring bolts of pain shooting from his own injured shoulder and forearm.

"痛い痛い！" came a yell from his subdued opponent, but Sev didn't hesitate. He pulled even harder, getting a better grip on the squirming arm. Yells turned into screams, comprehensible in every language. Something cracked; first it was the spacesuit's reinforced elbow joint, and then something snapped deeper inside. It was all over.

He let go, and his stalker immediately withdrew the mangled arm, crying like a helpless child. Sev exhaled, the pain and fatigue combo kicking in, but he couldn't rest just yet. He dragged himself over to the discarded crowbar and used it like a cane to prop himself up. *When did it all go so terribly wrong for us?* He gazed down at his shaking, powerless opponent curled in a ball under his feet. *We were supposed to rise as this unified human race, exploring and conquering Space with the power of our diversity, and yet here we are, muddled apes in the Space Age, still madly swinging makeshift clubs at each other's faces on distant planets. Where did we go so terribly wrong?*

He slowly lifted the rusty crowbar over his head, gripped it tightly with both hands and, with a primal shriek, finally brought it down on his opponent's skull.

***

An hour later he was still roaming around the empty hangar, his determination to leave the dead planet getting stronger with each painful step. The squatter that attacked him lay unconscious or dead –Sev didn't really care which – on the lower platform. Finding no spacecraft docked in this hangar, it became apparent that the trigger for the savage attack was a sight of a perfectly functional vehicle on the elevator platform, descending like a gift from the skies. Whoever the poor stranded soul was, he thought it could be his way out of here, and in a way – it was.

There were no spaceships docked in the Brusska station hangar, but it wasn't completely empty either. Repair bay was fitted with a pair of robust automated construction arms, as well as a functional assembly platform. And just before he got jumped, he observed an unfinished surface skimmer on one of the upper levels. After examining the frame, a practical idea formed in his mind. Even though the skimmer wouldn't be going anywhere, he could strip down the thruster components and convert his functional rover for spaceflight. Modular construction allowed for such experiments, as land and space-based vessels were built with interchangeable parts. By transferring a hydrogen tank to his MC rover and adding more thrusters, he could actually lift the heavy vehicle off the ground. Normally it would require a lot of work, but the robotic arms are here to help him splice the two vehicles into one.

That meant he would need to get rid of a lot of weight, but the same solid core design – built around two cockpits with a life-support system – could remain untouched. Refueling station had plenty of stored hydrogen, so that's one less thing to worry about.

Accessing the main computer grid, he set his plan into motion by transferring the skimmer chassis into the repair bay. He ordered everything to be disassembled, scrapped and stored inside the automated cargo holds. The speed with which the order was carried out was baffling. Construction frame held the chassis firmly in place, as two extendable robotic arms systematically grinded the joints of every module, swiftly handing the components to a waiting set of smaller servo arms that stored it in the utility chamber below, producing all sorts of mechanical clicks and sounds. Through a rain of sparks he observed the whole structure vanish before his eyes, saw-arms menacingly retracting like nothing happened. Witnessing the unrestrained power of machines was a frightening sight indeed.

Satisfied with the progress, Sev ordered the MC rover to be transferred from the elevator platform to the emptied repair bay. Blue lasers quickly mapped the whole vehicle, projecting every fine detail onto the control display. There he could see the weight, fuel and power distribution, and attempt radical changes on the virtual blueprint before unleashing the reconstruction operation. With such ease of operation, one would think spaceship construction is some kind of a game; but in reality, the lack of substantial knowledge could hardly be compensated. Massive components and lots of armor made the ship sluggish, so Sev removed both flank segments first. Then he deleted the wheels and the suspension, replacing them with advanced rotor-mounted thruster nozzles. The biggest problem was the hydrogen tank, a massive cylinder that would hold his fuel, and which had to be placed close to the center, in order to keep the ship balanced. He had to remove the cargo hold and widen the rear to make room for it, but overall he was happy that he made no structural changes to the original, tried and tested design.

After running a simulation and consulting the mass with the full tank, he realized he could still add a layer of light armor around the newly installed thrusters. Those vague mission instructions stated that he should 'intercept the merchant vessel Narwhal', but he still had no idea what kind of threat a trader could pose. Weapon systems will have to be added later, when things make more sense. He pressed the button to confirm his blueprint.

As the automated robotic arms disturbingly unfolded to surgically slice and convert a simple rover into a proper spaceship, Sev leaned on the fence and looked down to the elevator platform where the vagrant's body laid perfectly still. What a mess. What was his story? Another explorer left behind, who went crazy and feral over the years? The reason for such hostility on Mars eluded him. He could understand survival, but this was uncalled for. Maybe the madness was contagious and simply spreading through violence? *Was he looking at himself in a few years' time?*

So far, Sev's role on the red planet was that of an enforcer for a greedy crew on Earth that seemed utterly disconnected from the actual goings-on. In fact – the worse things got, the cheaper they could buy off all these failed space enterprises. Anger rose in his heart, but for now he left it unchecked, because he *needed it* to boil over.

9.   Waiting for the tribe

"Who *are* you?"

"Anokha."

"No, I mean, you are not from Ceres. Are you from Earth?"

She nodded cautiously.

"Wow. But... *how?* Where is your ship?"

Anokha turned her head away without replying. They were floating in what looked like a small, gloomy tunnel with no windows, the two of them barely fitting inside it. It felt like a service passageway, its walls lined with lights, wires and pipes.

"What is this place? Where are we?"

Iyor frowned, puzzled as to why his own question was ignored.

"You are safe. You are currently inside the Ceran miner bathyscaphe. It's not very comfortable, but it's better than being outside." He allowed that to sink in, observing her reaction. There was none. Anokha's face looked too tortured to reveal anything. "Would you like to rest now?"

"No." She said hesitantly. "I feel like I've been sleeping for days. I just need to cool down."

"Why did you cut off your suit's computer? Or did someone else do that to you?"

Anokha took in an invigorating breath of cool air. The top of her space suit was peeled back, revealing a sweat-soaked jumpsuit. *How long was she out there, hopelessly adrift?* She pulled one of the floating sleeves and looked at where her wrist computer used to be, frowning as if unsure what actually happened there.

"Were you attacked?" Iyor suggested.

"Yes." She said unconvincingly.

"Okay." Iyor nodded with a sigh of relief. "You were attacked by pirates in the Outskirts? I caught you floating from that direction."

Anokha's gaze wandered off, once again leaving him without an answer. The interior of this ship was uncomfortably small, resembling an escape capsule: two pilot seats below, surrounded by a wall of dark displays are forming a cockpit cradle. Everything is so small – as if it was built for kids.

For the first time she took a good look at her rescuer. But... he *is* just a kid! Slim, ribbed skinsuit developed by Ceres miners, clean shaved scalp and a tawny, sun-kissed skin contrasted by light-blue eyes. His body size was that of a child, but the face didn't seem so young, a web of tiny wrinkles already fanning out from those odd eyes. Floating in the gloom, he resembled an imp with strange, even slightly frightening features.

"Are you alright?" Iyor said, noticing the subtle change.

Anokha nodded a bit too fast. They floated in awkward silence for a few seconds, unsure where to go from here.

"Is this your ship?" Anokha started.

"Yes. Well, no. It belongs to my tribe. The rest of the guys are in Habakkuk base. They'll be back soon."

"So what happens now? Am I a prisoner?"

"No, what makes you say that? Earth did impose an embargo on us, but we are not enemies... I think. Life holds value here and having enemies is - expensive."

"That's a relief. For a moment I thought..."

"You can't stay here, though." Iyor interrupted her, resolutely.

"What do you mean?" Anokha frowned.

"Don't worry, I won't throw you out," he laughed, flooding the interior with his disarming, childish energy. "It's just that our tiny construction platform cannot provide for another person! We are generating barely enough energy, food and oxygen for the four of us. It's a fragile balance. When the rest of the guys return, we'll take you to Habakkuk and help you out. In the meantime – you can be our guest! Sounds good?"

Anokha's gaze turned glassy. She nodded absentmindedly, without replying.

"You are behaving strange, Anokha." Iyor tilted his head. "But... that's alright."

He pushed himself down into one of the seats, giving her some room. She found it comforting, but was still baffled at the wisdom this *child* displayed.

"You might want to buckle in that seat behind me. We'll head back to our construction platform. It's very spacious there," he said.

***

This is how I imagine Little Prince's planetoid would look like! Anokha thought upon seeing the tiny, silvery asteroid harboring the construction platform. The 'spacious base' was a single pressurized chamber with four globular sleeping modules branching off. Trinkets, personal items and even trash floated freely inside the main room. The degree of intimacy these kids are forced to share must make for a strong bond. She felt like an intruder in their little tree house. As soon as the suit was recharged, she suggested they should move back to the bathyscaphe and occupy themselves with some work on the unfinished cockpit cradle while they wait.

"Still no news from the rest of the tribe?" she asked carefully, breaking the silence.

"No news." Iyor said, seemingly unconcerned. "And we don't have any means of communicating over long distances. In fact, they are just bringing an operational antenna module for the base and this miner."

"How does that work – you barter the ore you dig for modules? And it feels strange to use the word 'tribe' in a spaceship, don't you think?"

"But that is our level, dictated by... the environment and lack of recourses, I guess. We can't afford to train specialists, so everyone does everything: each one of us is an engineer, a miner and a warrior. We all know how to pilot a ship. Each tribe receives a small nuclear reactor to power up the initial base, and then we turn in what we dig out for refining so we can order the components needed for expansion. Recently, we were all advised to add armor and weapon hardpoints to all utility vessels, so they can double as defense crafts for a joint fleet."

"You are expecting an attack? Who from?"

Iyor shrugged. "They wouldn't tell us to burden our craft with extra mass needlessly. Ceres ships are built for maximum efficiency – even though they look like space cucumbers." He laughed that childish giggle of his.

"How do you even know what a cucumber is? I'm sorry if that sounds rude, but I don't understand. I was warned that Cerans are some kind of space primitives, and yet I have no problem talking with you. You speak like you were born on Earth."

"Just give us time; we'll live up to your low expectations." Iyor chuckled. "But the answer is simple: we actually eavesdrop on Earth. A lot. Some of the words are only an abstraction for us, like 'rain', which we will never experience. Sometimes we mix up different languages, or make up our own words for stuff that you don't have, but in the end all our education comes from stray or pirated Earth transmissions. We fill the gaps with imagination and superstition. So I have an idea what a whale is, even though I'll never see one with my own eyes. The same is probably true for you to some extent."

"I see your point."

"But the communication is one sided." Iyor continued. "Nobody on Earth cares about anything going on around here. We are utterly forgotten."

Anokha thought about it as she was attaching another display on the pilot console. "So... if you know they don't care about you – why are you building a defense fleet?"

"Everybody retreated to Earth after the Big Expansion fizzled out, but for us this was a one way trip – we are already adapted to life in zero gravity. We can't go back to any planet. But the Grandmother Earth is a scornful lady. Why is there a ban on trading with us, hm? We would *die* if it weren't for the smugglers that bring in materials we simply cannot produce. Out here, there is no night and day, no respite from the radiation. Our average lifespan is below 30 Earth years, don't you know that? We can't make it out here alone, and they knew that when they walled us off."

"I..." Anokha fumbled for words, never really considering the impact her smuggling run might have. She was actually ashamed of exploiting the situation and thinking only of profit. And yet, there was something fishy about his story. "But still, it makes no sense. I think we both agree that no Earth mercenary fleet would attack Ceres, chasing you guys through this vast expanse that you are so familiar with, right? Knowing the current mindset of Earth corporations, they would consider it simply... unprofitable."

Iyor was strangely quiet, seemingly occupied with work.

Anokha frowned. "Hold on. You are not building a defense fleet. You are actually preparing for some kind of move. A *migration*..." she faltered, aware of her position.

Iyor didn't turn, but he obviously stopped with whatever he was working on. The cabin suddenly appeared smaller, and yet that airlock exit seemed so far away. Once again she fumbled for words: "I'm with you guys. I am a smuggler, an independent trader. I don't..."

When Iyor turned he wasn't smiling, a look of trouble on his childish face. "I have my own doubts about this weaponizing of our utility ships, but I was being honest in telling you what they have told us. You, on the other hand, feel no need to be sincere. I've provided you time to calm down, and I still have no idea who you are. What happened to your ship? I could be sheltering a failed pirate from the Outskirts, a Terran spy – or worse!"

Anokha bit her trembling lip, her gaze unfocused as if she is trying to remember something. Finally she said: "Your friends at Habakkuk. They... could be in trouble."

Iyor's eyes flashed with cold anger, a storm brewing up behind them. He rapidly pushed himself down into the pilot seat without saying a word, his silence *demanding* immediate answers. With hasty movements, he was powering up the ship for immediate launch.

"The pirate drone that followed my ship, I think both of them might be heading for the Habakkuk base now," Anokha forced herself to say. It was obvious to both of them that she was only telling half the story.

Iyor looked at her defiantly: "Habakkuk is well-protected by automated turrets and orbiting robot sentries, it will be safe from a single pirate drone. But why didn't you tell me this earlier? You know my tribe is there. Why are you *still* not telling me everything?"

Anokha looked away, silent. She was grateful that he displayed a dose of maturity, even though he was just a boy. With their brief lives, maybe they burn twice as bright, these Cerans.

"Let's get you to Habakkuk," Iyor said, laden with foreboding.

His gaze lingered on her mutilated wrist computer. An enigma, for now.

10.   Above the Red Planet

He landed on Mars to catalogue its mineral resources, measure it with Earth metrics and tame it for profit, but instead – almost three years later – he found *himself* being evaluated by the red planet. He arrived as an explorer, pushing that final frontier a little further, but now he was leaving it feeling like a simple drifter, harboring traitorous thoughts.

Mars arranged no hindrances for his departure. The polar gale seems to have died out, providing him the window of opportunity for a safe liftoff in his rover, now converted for space travel. The Clutter belt wasn't going to allow him safe passage, though. Made out of discarded components, thrusters, prematurely opened parachutes drifting like dead jellyfish, unfinished communication satellites, and other debris dragged all the way from Earth, or fabricated on spot, the littered exosphere of Mars stood as the biggest monument to human failure in the entire Solar System.

Unfazed, Master Control spaceship was blasting through this graveyard, shoving away bits and pieces with its thick armor. Sev felt each impact and heard the continuous hum of invisible dust-like particles sandblasting over the reinforced glass windows. It would be a perilous gamble to push further through the Clutter, where the risk of colliding with larger debris was too great; instead, he rolled his craft to be level with the shimmering yellow planet below, and continued toward the *Holiday Inn* checkpoint, a relatively safe passageway used by corporate automated ore-haulers. For this flight he was wearing a state of the art Navigator hood, a bulky addition to his helmet that displayed optimal vectors for entering various orbits, yellow and blue lines blazing like flaming highways through space. With his arm and shoulder still in severe pain, he felt grateful that the advanced hood also interpreted audio commands.

"Ship: Establish laser antenna connection with Apex satellite. Place a request for passage for an escort drone from *Holiday Inn* station; one ship designated 'MC', tonnage under 30, piloted by Superintendent Şevket Bulut of Apex Corp."

He had no idea which one of Earth's corporations or nations was the majority shareholder in *Holiday Inn* station at the moment, but placing an official request via Apex satellite should grant him passage, and the corporations can sort out the expenses amongst themselves. All payments were Earth-centralized anyway. It was all tit-for-tat; over the years, the ownership of various Mars ventures became too convoluted to follow. The *Inn* was still lucrative, though: the former hotel in areostationary orbit acted as a gate, refueling station, and sometimes even customs terminal before the automated cargo containers could be shipped to Earth. It was originally built as a resort, with its magnificent glass dome offering an unparalleled view of the red planet, but now it housed only truckers and a contingent of bored Navy personnel, a ragtag mercenary group that acted as a deterrent for pirates. Instead of repairing it, the splendid dome was scrapped down, after too many cracks appeared over time from all the flying junk. With the tourism days gone, the real benefit of *Inn* station today was its fleet of small, lightly armed drones, dubbed 'mosquitoes'. For a fee, one could escort you through the Clutter, tracking and intercepting any dangerous debris in your path. Automated turrets delivered kinetic projectiles, an old design with an upgraded cooling system still being the best tool for the job.

"Welcome, Apex pilot, this is the *Holiday Inn* station; you are approved for passage," came the reply, transmitted through a network of armored satellites. "Drone 5-72 is dispatched and on its way to the entry checkpoint."

"Copy that, *Inn*. I expect to reach the checkpoint shortly." He switched off the transmission.

"Ship: follow optimal course for *Holiday Inn* checkpoint. Place a request over Apex for a short term access to the local shipping traffic grid."

His expenditure approved, the head up display was updated

with a glowing layer of color-coded icons representing stations, ships, robots, satellites and even known debris all around Mars, detected through a relay of shared networks. The *Holiday Inn* base was also visible, but none of the Navy vessels appeared on this level of clearance. Still, the wider Mars area didn't seem as deserted as the surface. For some reason, that made him feel proud.

"Search: Independent merchant vessel *Narwhal.*"

Nothing.

"Search: science vessel *Vladivostok.*"

Again, nothing. Well, that was probably good news –he was either too early, or too late. He would have to check the traffic grid regularly and wait for any development in his mission plan. But first...

"Ship: roll 180. Switch off all internal lights."

With a painful groan he peeled back the Navigator hood and above him, in all its glory, Mars slowly rose into view –vast, cursed and... beautiful!

11.   Habakkuk, the ice base

"What did you do with my controls?" Iyor snapped, his command screen displaying a string of unfamiliar icons and options. They were sitting back to back in their pilot seats, but the distance seems to be growing between them, a strange discord stemming from the shared bond between the rescued and the rescuer.

"I've optimized the power distribution and linked various components, thus creating different modes of operation. It's a small programming addition that will help you get more out of the ship."

Iyor was silent for a while, as he tested the new functions. Simple, practical adjustments that made him think: *Why didn't I do that earlier?* The bathyscaphe, unfinished as it was, operated at times well over its power capacity, and Anokha's solutions remedied that.

"Where did you learn all this?"

"My ship taught me. It's a piece of junk held together by hotfixes." Anokha gave a strained smile. "That, and I graduated from the Lunar Engineering Academy, a family tradition."

"What's it like?" Iyor asked carefully.

"The Lunar Academy?"

"No. Family."

"What?"

"What's it like, having a family?"

Anokha found the question too simple to grasp. It was one of those things you took for granted. She struggled with an answer: "It's... like having a group of friends that will never give up on you. Crossing them would mean crossing the line – you end up hurting yourself."

Iyor was silent. A dark wall of screens enveloped them, compensating for the lack of windows in the cockpit cradle. The feed was brought in segments from cameras dotting the hull like black multifaceted gems. Some of it was zoomed in, some of it locked on and tracking who-knows-what; Anokha found it difficult to orientate, but the Ceran boy didn't seem to mind it as he gently directed the craft. Any minute now they should be approaching Habakkuk ice base, a remote bartering outpost.

"Do you see it?" Iyor asked, his voice trembling for some reason. "The shimmering..."

"What are you talking about?" Anokha scanned the displays, but found nothing of interest. Bathyscaphe was not equipped with sensors or radio equipment yet, so they were flying only based on Iyor's sense of direction.

"There is so many of them. What causes so much shimmering?"

"What shimmering? I can't see anything." Anokha unfastened her straps and turned around in her seat. All of Iyor's screens were focused on the distant ice asteroid ahead, and the multitude of little specks of light dancing around it. They blinked at regular intervals, like jewels in darkness. Are those...?

Crashing noises ripped through the cockpit, instantly bringing a smell of iron and smoke. Iyor instinctively rolled the bathyscaphe to the side, while Anokha regretted that she unstrapped her belts, sudden movement throwing her around the cockpit cradle, each wall impact feeling like a solid punch.

"Strap in! We are under attack!" Iyor screamed, as he tried to pull her back into the seat, piloting the craft with his other hand. "Try to locate the attacker! We have no sensors, so use the cameras. I'll keep evading, but it would help if I knew what."

That repetitive thunderous racket was the sound of heavy machinegun fire impacting over the hull. In the vacuum, their unfinished spaceship was a fragile bubble of air, and even a single projectile could pierce through and damage life sustaining components. Anokha was still bouncing around. Luckily, the tiny interior made it impossible to drift too far away, so she somehow clawed her way back into the pilot seat. Was she really doing this? Searching for an opponent with simple cameras? There's gotta be a better way.

"The worst part is," Iyor strained to talk, as he rolled the bathyscaphe to and fro, "I don't even know if we are still under attack. I can't hear anything until we are hit. Hurry up!"

"Working on it!" Anokha replied, as she activated focused beams of light to assist with the archaic visual search method. They had installed the ore detector module on the ship, so she rerouted some power to it, adjusted it for metal detection and tried to narrow the search area. Another short racket resonated through the hull and this time the sounds were different, as if they cracked something other than armor plates.

"There's your attacker!" shouted Anokha over the noise. "Tracking it with camera 5, with an added orientation overlay. Do you see it?"

"Yes." Iyor said calmly; bathyscaphe movements instantly became less erratic as he steered it to a wide turn.

"Turning off all unnecessary systems. You have full power for thrusters," yelled Anokha, way too loudly, agitated by that dreadful sound of gunfire. The 'attacker' was just a distant bright dot on one of the displays, with two flashing machinegun turrets spewing solid and tracer projectiles at them. Under Iyor's control, the bathyscaphe made a steady turn at reduced speed, thrusters finally blasting for a quick getaway right under their attacker. He risked a close distance snapshot but somehow he pulled it through, though for a second all displays flashed with an image of a symmetrical construct above them.

And then, there was nothing. All the displays turned black. All the lights– even the emergency ones – were out. Pitch black. Just for a moment, both of them thought the same thing: *Am I dead?* But one by one, the displays restarted: the unknown malfunction merely knocked them out temporarily. Even with their ship stunned, the momentum carried them through, so by the time enemy turrets turned around to catch up with them, they were already too far away.

"That was a *Ceran* guardian drone! Our own! It should be protecting Habakkuk. Why would it attack us?" Iyor said to himself. "And all that shimmering around the asteroid base... it's all pieces of debris. So many of them. Could a pirate attack cause such destruction?"

"No. I think it was caused by your own guardian drones," Anokha nodded, her mind slowly connecting the dots. "The same thing happened to my ship. Ever since I docked with Vladivostok, it was emitting some kind of interference that prevented it from detecting the owner. I tried to sabotage the antenna, just to stop the maddening transmission, but when I got out of the cockpit my own space suit was affected, forcefully receiving the commanding 'message' from Narwhal. All the microthrusters lit at the same time and jettisoned me off my ship! And then I couldn't think of anything better than to physically sever the connection, so I hacked off the communication computer from my wrist to stop the mayhem. By then I was already drifting blind, unable to catch up with the Narwhal. You cannot imagine how horrible that sound was!"

"We need to get them out of there." Iyor continued, as if he didn't hear her, his voice now weak. "We need to get in there and help. Habakkuk is... burning..."

Anokha tried to think of a way to reasonably present the folly of his plan. But instead, she bowed her head, overwhelmed by some strange guilt, as she heard him sob behind her.

"We *can* help!" she suddenly exclaimed. "Do you have a beacon around here? A navigation beacon, or a communication relay, anything that we can use to emit a one-way warning to stay clear of Habakkuk, and maybe round up all the survivors in one place?"

She felt the bathyscaphe immediately tilt into its new course, and wondered once again how he could navigate through space without complex computations and advanced sensors.

"There *is* such a place... the listening post that we use to eavesdrop on Earth transmissions!"

12. Vladivostok

Sev's communication with Apex Corporation, his employer, was unidirectional. All his reports were met with automated approval messages, as long as they fitted into prescribed budgets. Come to think of it, this was true of Earth in general. It was living in its own world, with refined ore coming in and orders pouring out. Initially, its orbital factories were pumping out ships and prefabricated modules for the Big Expansion, and it lasted... for as long as it was profitable. Space tourism, mining, philosophy, colonization, even missionary work – everything seemed to be expanding at the same time. Too bad it turned out to be so... hollow. When the profits declined, everybody started cutting their losses and retreated to Earth. Only the Ceres miners were left behind, stuck up there with nowhere to go back to, after decades spent adapting to a life without gravity.

Things still worked out for Earth, in the long run, but the thought that humans are a race meant to decipher all the mysteries of Cosmos seemed more distant now. Still, all this couldn't have been for nothing! The Big Expansion, the great bubble of aspiration bursting so... silently? He rejected the abstract idea of God, but he still had Faith. Seeds are sown and something, somewhere must take root and sprout, even in this harsh environment. He had to believe that, or his place among the stars held no meaning.

"Ship: Send encrypted report to Apex. *Mars orbit reached in an adapted, unarmed MC rover/spacecraft; awaiting arrival of Narwhal, Vladivostok, or further instructions. Brusska refueling base update – it contains no spaceships!*"

He spent the next two days in a rented capsule room on the *Holiday Inn* station, recovering from the scuffle he got into on his last day on Mars. *My last day on Mars.* The thought lingered in his mind.

Initially they've converted one wing of the old hotel to be a quarantine zone, but now it served as a capsule hotel for the traders. Basically, it was a truck stop. The central hub, shared with the Navy mercenaries offered Zero-G stripper shows with the glass floor overlooking Mars; that 'edge of the world' vibe attracting a loyal crowd of scurvy-bitten pardoned pirates, their grisly Navy counterparts and bored Earth traders: all of them glorified truckers, really. They spoke a multitude of languages, drinking and generally not understanding each other. Sev avoided the main Hub altogether, preferring quiet isolation to Earth scum, but the scene made his Faith waver.

He was lying in his bed, lulled by induced gravity of the revolving capsule hotel, when he received the message: *a craft designated Vladivostok was detected on the approach vector to Inn station.* He perked up, even though the order seemed wrong. He was expecting the Narwhal first, and then Vladivostok. Was he too late after all? In a matter of minutes, he was behind the controls of his MC spaceship, apprehensive and yet happy to see some progress.

"Ship: detach from dock and ping Vladivostok with laser antenna. If they respond, establish a dynamic link for communication."

Sev rubbed his gloved palms and checked the manual flight controls. Cockpit interior was left unchanged, with throttle lever and control wheel simply rewired to a new propulsion system. The ship responded well, but he still needed some time to get used to the lack of gravity.

Overhead display blinked green: a link established with the approaching vessel.

"This is MC... umm... spacecraft. Sev speaking. Apex summoned me to assist you. Vladivostok, could you please confirm that you hear me?"

"This is Vladivostok, Lero speaking. We hear you perfectly, Sev. Did you already manage to intercept the Narwhal transport?"

"Negative. I've been monitoring Mars space for two standard days." Sev sighed and then continued in a less formal tone: "I was told that you could provide me with more information, so – please tell me what's this all about?"

"We are victims of a simple theft," Lero spoke in a calculated manner. "Narwhal and its operator apparently stole large chunks of our research data during their last resupply visit. The problem is, you see, we operate in unregulated space, so..."

"...I think I understand." Sev sighed again. "You needed someone to strong arm the trader that ripped you off. But you're a freelance science vessel, how did you manage to involve Apex into this?"

"Oh, we reported to Apex that the data being stolen is theirs. Which is true. They hire us to do field tests and research for their various studies," Lero said cheerfully.

"I see. But we have a problem. Narwhal didn't pass through here. I even asked around this deplorable base here. Can you give me more info on the pilot?"

"Certainly. The pilot's name is Anokha Jágr, an independent merchant. We calculated Narwhal's trajectory based on our last contact with her, and confirmed that she was heading this way, but she could have altered her route. We noticed the theft almost immediately, but our systems were... I hate to admit it, but they seem to have been paralyzed by some sort of jamming signal acting as a smokescreen. It took us some time to purge the system, but we contacted Apex for help as soon as we reached the communication relay network. Although, we expected Narwhal to be here already."

"Jamming signal? Like a... computer virus?"

"It's not a virus, as there is no sign of replication. Instead, it was a very strong interference signal that temporarily knocked out most of our systems," Lero said calmly.

"Are you even sure that the data is stolen, and not simply

deleted?"

"There is a clear log of data being transferred from our ship to Narwhal, followed by obstructed communications and malfunctions on our side. It was rather unexpected, based on our previous assessment of Mrs. Jágr, but unfortunately we can only form our assumptions based on the evidence at hand."

"Hm... Jágr. An old naval family. They used to be big during the Expansion, but it seems they've fallen low, if they're running simple trade jobs. Well, it's obvious that Anokha has changed course, maybe for Earth or somewhere in the Belt. Is the stolen data valuable?"

There was a short pause from Lero's side: "Well, all we got is *you*, so..."

"Fair enough," Sev chuckled. "It makes even less sense to attempt a blunt attack for such an unpredictable payoff. But let's focus on finding out her whereabouts instead of her motives. We have Anokha Jágr either going rogue, or suffering a malfunction on her way here. How badly damaged are you?"

"Vladivostok suffered no structural damage, but for a while the ship behaved like there is no crew present on board, even putting the life support on hold. We manually cut off the power and restarted the core modules, reintegrating them one by one, but nothing seemed to work. After a while everything was back to normal, though, and the only lasting damage is simply the enormous amount of data we lost, so much so that we can hardly continue our work!"

"Alright. If you agree, our planned course of action would go like this: Keep Vladivostok far away from *Holiday Inn*, I don't trust anyone there. Place your ship in orbit around one of the moons. Apex can press the Jágr family on their end, see if they are somehow involved. And I will need the exact location of the incident, as well as the last calculated trajectory you have for Narwhal. Being a hauler, it can't be too nimble, so I can narrow down its possible trajectories.

And then we'll set a trap and get your data back."

13.   Assembling the Frame

"You have made me proud. Wrestling life out of this cold, harsh place. You have made me proud..."

With that, I attempted to say my farewell to Kali, Laszlo and Alber, but I have little experience with eulogies. All of them were missing after the collapse of Habakkuk base. For a very long time, I didn't allow myself a proper rest. Now if I leave my eyes closed for a second too long, I feel I would just fall asleep and drift away. Nothing seemed certain at this point. The fatigue was gnawing down my senses, sucking out all hope and exposing dark knots of pure misery. Somehow, I felt old and spent. Drifting aimlessly was nothing new, but now I couldn't even remember where I was coming from.

The mixture of gasses leaking inside the cockpit was plain bad. My head felt dizzy, and my throat was sore because of all the hydrogen from a punctured tank, as well as the cold seeping in through the damaged structure. Just one more sortie and then I could fully assess the damage and attempt repairs. One more sortie, skimming the outskirts of berserk drone patrols, looking for survivors and useful debris, but finding only corpses and shredded junk, scorched and useless. Just one more sortie.

But there were no survivors, only corpses with their suits ripped open, captured in perfect, grizzly poses, left to drift forever. I didn't dare disturb them, so I focused on undamaged modules that spun lazily in vacuum. Matter is the most important thing, one that can facilitate life. We were raised on transmissions coming from Earth, and yet there are some recurring motives in those that have always troubled us, subtle differences in our mindset, making us feel truly alien. We could observe no *resurrection* in space and no perfect circles, only infinite spirals leading nowhere, as everything was slowly moving away from everything else. Your dead body didn't automatically bring sustenance for plants and other life forms; it doesn't even decompose in vacuum, due to a lack of oxygen. Ashes remain ashes, dust stays dust. There was no alchemy of soul, only perfect stasis as you got mummified– for eternity. The only thing we could repurpose are bits of assembled matter. As I flew through chunks of rock and ice, dispersed like tears by the explosion, I saw so much shimmering, so much destruction. *Sometimes, you just squander what you are given.* My thoughts were convoluted, weariness and toxic fumes painting a dark prophecy for all of us...

While I count the dead, we agreed for Anokha to stay and round up the living on the listening post, a small station used to eavesdrop on Earth communications. Together, we hastily converted it into a beacon, emitting a message for all possible newcomers to avoid Habakkuk, and for all possible survivors to head towards us in radio silence. We have no idea what exactly we are up against, in this newfound reality of being unrecognizable to our own constructs.

But as I finished my final scavenging run with a tow of useful modules, I could see dozens of ships already docked at our makeshift beacon base– somebody heard our call! Other tribes will join in, and in spite of it all, we *will* mend the pieces together, refusing to give in to the void.

***

"Contact-based dynamic connection established. This is Tenesha, tribe of six. Who do we have here?"

"Edra, tribe of fourteen."

"Leif, speaking for Eris, still missing along with two others. Used to be a tribe of seven."

"Rogue, tribe of four."

"Keira, tribe of six."

"Iyor, speaking for the missing Kali. Tribe of four."

Anokha couldn't help but notice that all the voices were young, and all of them were female except for the two who were speaking for their missing tribeswoman. The rescue beacon on the listening post attracted other miners, but they just circled at first, wary of some kind of trap. They must have seen what they call 'the shimmering' in the direction of Habakkuk base, because they finally approached and docked. Upon finding her inside the listening post wearing a Terran space suit, they quickly flashed small, claw-like karambit blades and barraged her with questions. With Iyor away, she remembered to present herself as a smuggler breaking the embargo and was immediately met with a friendlier face. When Iyor returned, they found the capsule-like room of the listening post too small to fit all, and assembled this closed circuit communication to plan their next move. It was cold inside Iyor's bathyscaphe, thermal protection damaged or never properly installed. They shivered.

"Let's keep this brief, since every second counts. We are the first to pick up on your beacon, but many more will surely come. What is going on with Habakkuk? The smuggler pilot tells us that our own drone robots are running amok," said one of the voices.

"That is correct; we were attacked by a sentry drone as soon as we got close to what's left of the base. We saw no other enemies; however, we weren't able to scan properly." Iyor replied, his voice raspy and tired.

"Yes, what is this about radio silence? Is it to avoid detection?"

Iyor swallowed hard. "It's... something else. According to Anokha, the smuggler whose cargo ship is also trapped at Habakkuk, there is something interfering with all computer systems, and it's probably being transmitted and received by regular communication and radar channels. We have no idea what could be its origin. However, we experienced a brief shut down of systems during a fly-by with the rogue drone."

Anokha raised her brow. Sitting back to back, she could not see Iyor's face as he delivered the report, but the obvious omission of Narwhal's possible role as the source of interference was welcome.

"Could this be an attack by Terrans, or Horsemen pirates?"

"We don't know yet, but we have to get to Habakkuk, even if it means going through our own drones. There could be survivors! My tribe is still trapped there!" Iyor cried out.

"There is no Habakkuk," interrupted the one previously introduced as Edra. "The base is blown to bits by explosions; we can see it from here. Habakkuk was sitting on hydrogen fuel tanks. It is time to cut our losses and m..."

"Well, I'm going in alone, even without your support!" Iyor spit out through his teeth.

Unfazed, Edra continued: "You don't understand. Of course we will join you in an attempt to rescue our trapped brothers and sisters, but we should not be fooled by the idea that we can repair or rebuild something as complex as Habakkuk. Without the refinery module, food farms and fuel tanks, it's just a huge chunk of stone and ice. Our numbers have grown in this sector, and thousands of Cerans have begun to depend on this station. Even with all the bits and pieces we could salvage, many will suffocate and die before we can rebuild it. We need to move as one, while our supplies still hold."

There was hollow silence after Edra delivered her grim perspective.

Finally Tenesha, the woman who initiated the assembly, spoke with unease: "I see your point, Edra. And with the embargo, we cannot even ask for help from Earth in these hard times – but where could we go from here? We can't move back to Ceres! This would strain the Mother Base to its limits, maybe even bring about its downfall. We could spread into uninhabited reaches or retreat to other sectors, mitigating the damage, but only the shortsighted would take this path. We cannot afford to fall back on our own! They would probably defend against the intrusion, which would turn us into pirates that cannibalize everything we have assembled so far."

"Perhaps we will think quicker once we start running out of oxygen. A new equilibrium will eventually set in after all this destruction," Edra prophesized in a grim tone. "But let us focus on getting through our own berserk sentrybots first. No matter what the smuggler claims about the sensors, I will not be going in there without a radar to guide my missiles."

Anokha shook her head in disbelief. Stubborn kids. They will charge in there with no hope of success.

"We managed to evade those tracking machinegun turrets with steady turns at high speed." Iyor spoke excitedly, obviously blind to the danger faced with the prospect of saving his tribe. "Our ship is unarmed, but with less mass we can speed up ahead of you and draw their fire."

"This is Anokha, pilot of the lost cargo ship Narwhal." With her finger on the button, she decided to interrupt this children's tea-party. "This is madness. You cannot go in there with sensors and operational antennas. Don't you understand that's what caused the sentrybots to go haywire in the first place? Once you get close enough, your commands will freeze and you'll find yourselves trapped inside an unresponsive hunk of metal. I've been there. That's what happened to me! And your plan of diverting their fire wouldn't work either, as automated turrets prioritize armed targets. Going in there is just... futile."

"And yet we'll still do it. There is a higher cause in recklessness," Edra said, calmly, as if proclaiming some tribal dictum, "that is how we managed to colonize a good part of asteroid belt." This was met with silent approval from the others.

"Alright, we will form up around Edra's missile bathyscaphe. Disable all dynamic communications. Set to passive sensors and focus on intercepting enemy rockets. Remember that we also have two dangerous rogue missile sentrybots there; we can only hope we don't run into them on our approach," Tenesha concluded.

"This is stupid." Anokha grumbled, without bothering to press the button.

"Anokha, please stay behind on the listening post. Others will be coming soon, and they will help you out. But I must go. My tribe is... my family."

"Like hell you are going in there alone! Start those thrusters."

***

They were going in fast, clumped in a tight formation – as if huddling together would shield them from this dreadful place. Six bathyscaphes of similar shape, but different size and loadout, advanced through burnt debris toward the huge asteroid looming in the distance. They chose speed over maneuverability as their tactic, leaving a trail of red taillights. Auto-targeting computers could easily predict the movement of any object, but with the relatively slow projectiles still in use, they would need to be moving on the same vector as their target for a solid hit. Dogfights in space were still largely a mystery, and simple calculations and not valor were better suited for long distance, high speed confrontations. The toxic mixture of gasses inside their cockpit cradle was becoming unbearable, so both Iyor and Anokha were forced to breathe from their suits' supply of oxygen.

"Anything?" Iyor mumbled, bloodshot eyes nervously skipping from one display to another.

Anokha shook her head: "Debris. Lots of it. Was Habakkuk a large base?"

"Yes, it... was. Not nearly as big as Ceres, but it served as a production center and storage hold for all the tribes in this sector, as well as a docking gate for smugglers. It's incredible; I can see whole sections of the base that I visited just a few days ago. They are just drifting there, riddled with bullets. I think nobody was prepared for an attack that had no other purpose than simple destruction. With

Horsemen pirates you can be sure that they would try to disable and snatch modules undamaged, not just wreck everything. This level of destruction is... inhumane."

"I know the feeling," Anokha nodded. "A machine gone wild resembles a force of nature. It's just simple matter in motion, but the fact that we assembled it – that human imprint makes it appear more sinister. "

With so much shifting debris and sunlight struggling to get through, it was difficult to discern any menace that could be hiding out there, and as they got closer to the asteroid it became increasingly apparent that no attack will come at all. There was no sign of sentrybots, or any other operational ship. A huge dark crater scarred the surface of the asteroid where the base used to be, jagged edges like teeth exposing an icy core from which steam billowed, like the maw of Hell. On one of the displays Edra's large bathyscaphe swayed rhythmically, signaling to everyone that they will circle the whole asteroid, still on high alert.

They cruised around the murky rock, nerves jumping with each suspicious movement, yet still they found nothing, and nothing had found them in this dismal graveyard; there was no sign of defense drones or the Narwhal, not even as a broken wreck.

***

They came in packs, attracted like moths to the flames of Habakkuk. Ceran bathyscaphes, crude towing barges, mining and salvaging ships appeared from the void, hundreds of small tribes gathered to witness the death of their base. There was even a brief moment of hope, when some wild-eyed survivors were found on a damaged escape capsule. They delivered a report of disaster nobody really wanted to hear, confirming the collapse was quick, terrible and confusing. It's like all systems unhinged simultaneously, and then they were under attack by their own sentrybots. There was an explosion, so intense it altered the orbit of the whole asteroid. No more survivors were ever found.

The danger had passed, or just wandered away, and Habakkuk was now a cloud of pieces slowly spreading out around the cracked icy asteroid. Crews slept in shifts, but their ships worked without pause, collecting the broken bits to be sewn onto what they called the Frame – a chaotic patchwork of damaged modules temporarily welded together to the listening post. They worked zealously, and they spoke very little, but behind those tired, silent eyes some new, hellish energy was boiling; it commanded them to retaliate, but their enemy was unknown and it was inevitably going to get a lot worse when the supplies start running out.

Anokha and Iyor did their best to contribute in those initial rescue operations, until extreme exhaustion finally knocked them out. Much later, waking up to a freezing temperature and funky air in the cockpit, they found themselves dazed and with pain in the joints.

"Anokha..."

"I'm awake."

"Anokha, I..."

"I'm sorry about what happened, Iyor. About everything."

"It's... not over. It's never over. Kali told me this some time ago. And now Edra claims that this is the work of some Shimmering God of destruction, a glorious sign that will serve as a catalyst for all Cerans to unite and move forward."

Anokha was quiet, so he changed the subject: "Still no trace of your ship?"

"Nothing yet."

"I don't know what's going to happen next. My tribe's little construction platform can provide some food and power, but it's not... it's not how it should be. Edra wants to lead everyone as refugees, but armed ones. Like those augurs of old, she says that we are doomed, but at least we can help other Cerans by blockading

Mars cargo routes, and thus forcing Earth to withdraw the embargo."

Anokha said nothing, so he continued: "I am not sure what to think of it. Current alignment makes Mars closer to us than Earth, so we can be there before them."

"That's all right," Anokha said in a disinterested tone.

They were sitting in silence, illuminated by a wall of displays showing dozens of ships busy towing bits of scrap for the people in spacesuits to weld onto a shaky rectangular construction around them. Iyor waved and the displays turned off.

"What about you, Anokha? There is certainly room for a Moon Academy navigator on this migration to Mars."

"No." Anokha replied sternly. "I know my options here are limited without a ship, but I will not be the one to lead this children's crusade of yours."

"It's not like that. I am not even sure I like the idea of taking part myself. Moving to Mars would mean war, no matter how they sugarcoat it."

"Mars is named after a god of war, he wouldn't mind."

Iyor chuckled a bit. It was a relief to hear that childish giggle fill the cockpit once more, even though it ended with a cough: "So, do you have a better plan, Anokha?"

"Yes. I will wait for a chance to steal this fast bathyscaphe of yours, and head to Mars in an attempt to stop this madness before it's too late."

Iyor chuckled some more, but was soon invaded by coughing spasms: "An awesome plan! Do you mind if I help you with it?"

Anokha unbuckled her seatbelt and stretched in her seat. Their bathyscaphe was currently latched onto the revolving Frame base, and a small amount of induced gravity made things easier inside the crammed cockpit. She turned around to face the odd boy.

"Iyor, what I'm about to tell you could turn out to be important," Anokha begun in a serious tone. "I was frantically searching for a trace of my hauler among the debris, and I've found nothing! Same goes for your sentrybots. They are gone but– they are not destroyed."

Iyor blinked. "But where are they?"

"Even though I got separated from it, my ship continued its journey – and autopilot brought it to Habakkuk. Then: *Bam!* Your defense drones turn on you. As soon as its batteries were recharged, it must have went on towards its next stop, a trajectory calculated to take full advantage of the current alignment of Mars and Earth, its final stop."

"So the ship is on autopilot, destination Mars? But where are our sentrybots?"

"At first I thought Vladivostok was to blame, and I am still certain they had something to do with it, but now I am beginning to think that Narwhal could be the actual source of the interference signal. I observed a pirate drone being remotely pacified and forced to escort it, and I can find no better explanation except that your defense robots also succumbed to this effect. Now this little fleet – consisting of a cargo hauler from Earth, and its drone slaves – is zooming towards Mars. If we don't stop it – another Habakkuk will happen there. And then another one on Earth. Edra's shimmering god of destruction might be a real thing after all."

Iyor nodded slowly, this tangled moment unlocking a new universe full of possibilities branching out from different decisions. Overwhelmed, his mind raced to label different outcomes as good or bad, and even looked at it from different perspectives: would Cerans benefit from chaos at Mars, could the Narwhal even slip away to Earth and isn't that what the hungry ghosts of revenge really wanted, deep down? As possibilities started to fold, twist and coil around each other, there came a brief moment of clarity when he thought of nothing at all, and the words came out.

"We will race this rogue fleet to Mars and put this mechanical deity to the test."

Second segment: Breaking the long Silence

Future might be shaped by warriors, dreamed by poets, measured by scientists and interpreted by philosophers, but when everything hangs in balance, they will all wait to hear what the most important one among them has to say – the traitor.

— *Betrayer's rant*

1.   Burglary at Deimos moon

Dark, distant shapes passed beneath them. Holding hands and flying abreast only in their space suits, the two of them advanced steadily toward their target, the irregular surface of Deimos crawling far below, and a watchful scarlet planet reflected on their visors. In their free hands each of them held a heavy duty grinder, and on their chests – attached with a magnetic pin –gleamed a steel karambit knife, a primitive tool ideal for slashing spacesuits. Thanks to a careful deployment they've managed to place their bathyscaphe in a fragile orbit directly opposite from their target, hoping the miniscule moon would hide their presence. Now they left their unarmed spacecraft for a spacewalk that would allow them to approach without detection. Behind the misshapen horizon of Deimos a tuning-fork shaped spaceship was slowly rising, its green service lights blinking peacefully.

"That is Vladivostok," Anokha whispered on the repaired datalink. "Are you scared, Iyor?"

"I am," her child companion replied. "There is another craft docked with it."

"How can you even see that?" She squinted, but couldn't make out anything; space-born Cerans really had extraordinary vision. "Prepare for landing."

Holding hands during deceleration turned them into a single compact object, as bluish micro thrusters of their spacesuits flickered to life. Vladivostok was growing before their eyes, a huge symmetrical vessel painted in black and white. Now Anokha could see a small, ocher-colored spaceship docked on one of its connectors, right where Narwhal used to be moored recently. Recently? So much has happened, and time wasn't a proper medium to measure it. But who was this visitor? Two-pronged fore section of Vladivostok was spinning steadily: "There! At the tip of the prong, that's our way in. Do you see it?"

Iyor's mind was set on landing them safely. Were they coming in too fast? It was difficult to properly judge the distance with such a large object, so he focused on the man-sized yellow airlock door at the tip of the revolving section, and corrected their trajectory to intercept it, while nervously looking for any sign of automated defense turrets on the hull. Anokha assured him there were none, but when you're undertaking a free-space burglary, words are hardly enough. As they approached the airlock door, they let go of each other and latched onto the handrails, immediately feeling the gentle pull of induced gravity.

"Quickly! Before they realize we are here!" Anokha ordered, but found it difficult to orientate and move.

Iyor was quicker to adapt. He landed soundly on the doorstep, connected the grinder tool to his suit's power and started to work on a small keypad next to the door, creating wild yellow sparks that didn't know where to go. Every module came with its own computer terminal, and Iyor was good at hacking his way into it, albeit in a rather unsophisticated manner; he removed the front panel and simply replaced the exposed chipset with a new one he brought with him. Then he accessed the keypad without even bothering to reassemble the floating circuitry, and the airlock door obediently opened, revealing a small illuminated chamber, its walls lined with spacesuits. He managed to break inside before Anokha could subdue her embarrassing weakness by shifting her perspective. Mumbling her Zen mantras she followed Iyor inside, allowing the airlock door to reseal silently behind them, instantly pumping air and sounds inside.

"We're in," Anokha stated the obvious, just to buy herself some more time.

Iyor looked around the room. Even when he opened the visor of his helmet to better hear the sounds, everything seemed quiet; no footsteps or alarms could be heard. His suit power was low, drained from a long spacewalk, but they already knew this would be a one-way trip. During their approach to Mars they've made a brief stop to hack into a communication array, learning the locations of all the spaceships around the red planet, and Anokha was very surprised to see Vladivostok orbiting around the Deimos moon. She took it as a clear sign that they are somehow involved, so she and Iyor jumped at the chance to learn more, before Narwhal and her fleet of rabid drones arrive, bringing mayhem to the entire sector.

"Lero's room should be down the main hall. I can't wait to squeeze some answers out of that slimy bastard."

"This could get messy. You said you spent some time on this station-ship; how many scientists are on board? I see four spacesuits here."

"Yes, there should be four of them, plus that little ship we've seen docked. We ought to be careful."

Iyor nodded, arming himself with a knife, discarding the heavy grinder tool, and it was slightly worrying that Anokha clung to hers. All was still quiet and smelled faintly of ozone when they opened the door, revealing a long hallway illuminated by dim lights. Swiftly they pressed on, passing doors which led to sleeping quarters, kitchen and green-lit oxygen farm. Finally, Anokha stopped in front of a simple interior door. They exchanged looks and nods in silence, before pressing the button.

Lero's room was spacious, with a narrow window on the far wall and a computerized oblong desk with rulers, set of protractors and a high-tech 3D compass scattered around what looked like a computerized star map. Most importantly, Lero was present, his gaunt figure with bushy grey hair bent over the table. He looked up to face the intruders and slowly lowered his magnifying monocle in pure amazement, but he couldn't do much as they fell on him like a duo of practiced hunters; Iyor pulling him down from the chair even though the man was twice his height, while Anokha loomed over them with a buzzing grinder in hand, face void of any emotion. She wasn't even acting – she truly felt nothing at this point, not even anger.

"I...I...Anokha?! Is that you? What... what are you doing here?"

The old man didn't fight back, as Iyor clung to him like a monkey with wicked fire burning in his eyes. Neither of them bothered to provide any answers.

"Hey, let's be reasonable here...um... er..."Lero attempted again, but found it hard to finish his plea, utterly scared.

Finally, Anokha spoke: "We are looking for answers, Lero. What have you done to my ship? What happened at Habakkuk station?"

"I don't know! You are clearly out of your mind! Sev, do something!" the old man squealed.

For the first time, they looked around the room. They got tunnel-vision upon seeing their target, so they didn't notice another man standing next to the sleeping chamber in the far corner of the room. He was wearing a dusty spacesuit with a bandolier slung over its shoulder, his short beard and unkempt hair adding to his rugged-but-stern look.

He spoke slowly, with an unflinching gaze fixed on Anokha: "We seek answers as much as you do, so... let's talk. But if things get ugly– so will I."And with that he lifted up a compact, high caliber rifle: a standard model that could deliver plenty of punishment, with little to no fear of stray bullets piercing the spaceship hull.

"Who's this goon, Lero? What have you gotten us into?" Anokha glowered at him suspiciously.

"That is Mr. Sevket from the Apex Corporation, and he is here to help. I share his sentiment: let us talk as equals."

Sev raised his chin, as if assessing the situation, and then slowly ejected the magazine from his rifle.

***

Soon they were seated with Lero's geometry tools, Sev's weapon and Anokha's grinder scattered on the same computerized desk. Iyor kept his distance, leaning on the wall and starring out through the narrow window slit, as if longing to be out of this room. Sev was rocking in his chair, arms crossed and eyes closed, processing the heated exchange between Anokha and the scientist.

"There was something in there that infected my ship, and brought havoc on Habakkuk! Don't tell me you don't know what it is."

"But, I don't know, Anokha! Everything went haywire on our side, just like during our last conversation, you know? We experienced a blackout that threatened the lives of everyone on board, and when we recovered, a good chunk of our data was gone. What were we to conclude from that?"

"I didn't steal anything! I went through the logs and found out a massive load of some self-encrypting data housed in the..."

"Self-encrypting you say?" Lero interrupted.

"Yes, the immense processing data needed for the shifting encryption leeched most of my modules' computing power."

"Interesting..."

"It's not *interesting*, Lero. Habakkuk base is space-rubble now because of it, and Narwhal will soon be here. Cerans are thinking about following its trail of destruction."

Sev stepped in, as if to defuse the situation: "Did the encryption give you some kind of clue about what's going on, Lero?"

"Possibly. What do you know about radio telescopes?" the graying scientist asked, unfazed by Anokha's tone.

Everybody stared blankly.

"Initially they built huge ones back on Earth and, while they could make them as large as a valley, there was constant interference from existing signals: radio, television, radars... They thought it would be ideal to build one on the far side of the Moon, where they could listen to the stars in silence – and they did, but then Moon bases started sprouting, and soon it wasn't silent anymore. So they built them behind Mars, but then it got colonized as well..."

"Hah! Colonized? More like economized," Sev snorted.

"Whatever, my point being: the radio clutter was already introduced, and they kept building them further and further away from the radio pollution. There were multiple incidents when a confirmed 'transmission from aliens' turned out to be just a secret military satellite prowling through some far corner of the Solar system."

Anokha sneered: "What's this got to do with anything? Radio telescopes are obsolete, nobody uses them anymore."

"Correct. And yet, abandoned as they are – they are still out there, listening. Hearing is a peculiar sense, one you cannot turn off. You can easily shut your eyes, but you can't close your ears. After the Big Expansion seeded dozens of these radio telescopes further and further away, there was an almost unexplainable drop in interest and funding for space exploration – and even science in general. Vladivostok is a freelance science vessel precisely because there's no constant funding, need I say more? Everything is outsourced, even research. Recently, private corporations started buying off empty colonies, mining concessions and anything they could grab at an all-time low price."

"Vultures, picking bones from a corpse." Sev groaned, and Anokha looked at him, surprised to hear such disloyalty from a company man.

"But at first it did feel like a renaissance of sorts, a revival of old entrepreneurship that spawned the Big Expansion, didn't it?" Lero smiled, reminiscing.

"At first, yes." Sev nodded. "But from what I've seen on Mars, it seems as if Space affairs are currently in the hands of hungry accountants. That's not right. My company, for example, just keeps buying and scrapping assets, with no investment at all. And they are turning profit, even in this recession."

"Exactly. And that's exactly what Apex did, when they bought off the closed French national space agency assets throughout the Solar System, old radio telescopes included. They've sent us to pick up the jalopies, take them apart, and construct a communication relay to be leased for automated mining operations on Europa. We did this, but found years' worth of data collected by the telescopes. Apex told us to transfer all of it, and that they will find the buyer on Earth – but there was one batch of collected data that was secured with an alternating encryption like we've never seen before. We couldn't copy or delete it, so we kept the original databank module on Vladivostok, and waited for Apex to press someone from the closed French agency for the data key."

Anokha tilted her head: "Maybe this encrypted data 'escaped' to my ship as some sort of anti-theft measure set by the French agency?"

"Well, here's the thing..." The scientist paused intentionally. "Apex reported that they have spoken with previous owners, and there wasn't supposed to be any encryption at all."

Sev frowned: "So? Radio telescopes are open to all sorts of signals; maybe they picked up some military communication and stored it?"

"My people believe it is a word of God. A shimmering herald of destruction."

They all turned to face the star-child, but Iyor kept looking through the window as if he said nothing.

"Word of God? There could be some truth in this."Lero's eyes raced over the room, as if calculating something.

"You can't be serious!" Anokha protested.

The scientist looked back cheerfully. "Why not? What appears to us as some sort of divine encryption that messes up our computers, could simply be the work of advanced technology, picked up as a transmission emanating from beyond our Solar System, long ago. That is what radio telescopes were used for, after all: listening for an echo of intelligence in the sky."

"Errr... aliens and gods?" Sev said, with a mocking smile.

Lero shrugged: "Long dead alien god, yes. It's either that, or the French have lost the data key and they're simply too embarrassed to admit it."

Stupefied, they were sitting in silence, when a priority notification dawned on the surface of the computerized desk.

PUBLIC SECURITY WARNING ISSUED BY SECTOR CONTROL: EARLY DETECTION PLATFORM FAILED.
NAVY VESSELS DISPATCHED TO INTERCEPT POSSIBLE PIRATE THREAT.
CAUTION ADVISED FOR ALL CIVILIAN AND CORPORATE VESSELS!

2.   The report that was never sent

"I have to admit, I don't feel any wiser."

Staring out the window, I recently found myself talking to whatever lies on the other side. There was *nothing* out there, and it's a good listener. My room here on Vladivostok was filled with luxuries: for starters, it had plenty of space, a hammock bed, induced gravity, and the most amazing thing of all – this little window! It's so pleasantly inefficient, this thing. My face was so close that drops of condensation started to form over its cold, perfect surface. Outside, the stars seemed to be constantly falling, as the entire fore section of the ship revolved, inducing a mild push. Every minute or so I could see Anokha and Sev working outside, their welding tools shining like fireflies in the night as they were assembling a rocket launcher module. They were on some kind of a warpath ever since that public security warning was issued a few hours ago, and assembling weapon modules seemed to give them some kind of relief. We were still waiting for updates from the Navy.

My bathyscaphe was now joined with Vladivostok in orbit around Deimos, the smaller and more distant of the two moons of Mars. Along with what looked like a converted rover, we now had a small fleet of mixed allegiances. For a company man, this Sev seemed to be quite disillusioned. Something on Mars made him lose his way, or maybe it was just the sheer distance from home that slowly cracked him? He wasn't saying much.

Even Anokha was in a strange mood. She's been fighting with the fact that she was kicked out by her ship, and has nowhere to return to without it. Accusing her of theft seemed to have upset some deeply rooted moral code and high standards imprinted by her family. For all intents and purposes it is as if she was never really rescued: still floating out in the void, with nothing to cling to.

And me? I wonder how *I* feel. There seems to be a path set

before me with these two, but what worries me the most is this newfound sense of security, a brazen idea that no matter how bad things seem to be going–they will never *stop* going, and I found some perverse comfort in that. But the meaning, the purpose of it all eluded me, and I don't feel any wiser, smarter or richer. We can admire things like a perfect sunrise, growing up and expansion, but–like the beat of some cosmic heart –it's all followed by its opposite. That's how I felt: contracted. I couldn't wait for what comes next.

***

"It's sunny today," Sev said in a serious tone, which made the joke even funnier.

Anokha chuckled without looking at him. Welding tools in hand, they were assembling four launcher tubes housing simple, non-tracking rockets. The unfinished module was temporarily fixed to Vladivostok's wide hull, as they weren't sure which one of the two small ships they had will carry it. It *was* sunny today, and the *day* will never end out here, not in their lifetime. Beneath them the dead surface of Deimos crawled steadily, the occasional glimpse of long forgotten crashed probes giving it an appearance of a cosmic graveyard.

"Do you think the Navy will heed our warning, Sev?"

"We must break the silence, no doubt about it. But will they listen? I don't know. They will get mighty suspicious of us, though. It's a tricky situation, but if your calculation is true, Narwhal should be here in a few hours, unless the Navy manages to disable it. They *are* our best chance at stopping it. Don't you think so?"

Sev looked up from the launcher tube he was assembling, and noticed her troubled face through her visor.

"I guess." Anokha replied, with a blank face.

"I understand we are talking about disabling, maybe even destroying your ship, Anokha, but if it is behind the disaster in the asteroid belt..."

"It must be stopped, yes. I understand."

Sev didn't take his eyes off her, and saw that despite her resolute words, her mind was divided as ever.

"Not to mention those dead alien gods, eh?" she attempted to lighten up the conversation.

"Do you believe there could be some truth in that?" Sev said, sincerely fascinated.

"We have no proof for – or against – that theory. It's just that poking to get some proof is so damn dangerous. In the end, it doesn't matter." she shrugged. "My suit is dry. I'll head inside and order the production of more parts for other weapon modules. I'll meet you there, and we can finally send out that warning to the Navy."

He waved her goodbye, and watched as she gracefully flew toward the airlock section of the lean black and white spaceship constructed for deep space operations. Without her company, his dark thoughts closed in. For a few moments he was just drifting there doing nothing, holding an unfinished rocket tube and a bright lit welder tool in his arms, when he was overtaken by a vague feeling that he was being watched. Finally he made up his mind, attached the segment he was working on to the long, oblong launcher, and then set aside his tool. He glanced around, and felt the mirrored windows of Vladivostok look accusingly at him.

Slowly he made his way around the hull of the science vessel, until his own little MC spacecraft came into view, moored with the connector ring. Moments later he was inside the familiar cockpit, checked his timepiece and pulled on the Navigator Hood. It was time.

"Ship: establish laser antenna datalink with the Apex satellite."

"Satellite in position. Datalink active, no new messages," the ship reported after a few seconds.

"Prepare report for Apex Corporation: Established contact with Vladivostok. I have the captain of the Narwhal in custody. The Narwhal itself and the stolen data are still missing, presumed to arrive shortly into Mars orbit with chances of retrieving them intact very slim."

He paused, struggling to continue.

"Additionally – there are reports from the asteroid belt that a destroyed Ceran base triggered a violent migration fleet, jeopardizing all company assets here. Further communication with this sector of Mars potentially compromised. Provide immediate assistance!"

He just needs to utter the word 'Send', and everything should be alright. His job and countless lives depended on this precious warning.

"Abort. Delete the whole report."

And with that, he betrayed the company – and so much more.

3.   An alliance

No matter how much the four of them glared at it, the 'no network' icon wouldn't go away.

"We were too late in our attempt to issue a warning, as most communication relays have fallen into silence," Lero brooded.

Sev tilted his head: "Or maybe the Navy received our message, and caused a blackout in the sector. But, without any notice? That would be strange."

Iyor kept silent as usual, but this time he looked with great interest at the black horizontal panel displaying Mars, its two moons and dots and triangles representing the last recorded location of various ships and stations in the sector. The whole image was faded and frozen, due to a lack of network connection.

"Frankly, I have a feeling we were divided on our decision to warn them in the first place." The scientist looked Anokha in the eye: "We must stop your ship without any further delays, Anokha. The chain of events is causing more misery with each passing moment. We could be labeled as traitors when this is all over."

Iyor smiled, his face illuminated by the screen: "We are not the traitors here. We are the ones trying to *put down* a rebellion of our traitorous machines."

They all looked at him, astonished. Iyor stared down, embarrassed at all the attention he was getting: "See, this is why I rarely speak, because every time I open my mouth, you look at me like I'm some prodigy."

"No, you're right. We have to look at the big picture here." Sev nodded. "But how can we achieve what the Navy obviously failed to do? They have – or *had*– a full squadron of heavy corvettes with plenty of firepower. What went wrong?"

"The innate fallibility of their construction betrayed them," Lero spoke in a lecturing manner. "All the ships after the Big Expansion share the same modular construction, parts are interchangeable, they can be reused – it's all great and cost efficient, but they also share the same weaknesses. This unknown hi-tech interference knocked out all of their systems without resistance. They were ready for pirates, but not for something like this."

"Are *we* ready?" Sev said. "I have a problem with this *alien signal* theory."

"Then dismiss it." Anokha moved in. "I mean, call it whatever you want. I call it *Clang*, after the initial noise it made on my ship. Don't get me wrong, I have no reason to believe it myself, but you've spent years in space, right? You must see the universe as something that can easily house numerous possibilities – even life!"

"I've spent years exploring Mars, and it quickly became obvious that life never developed there, and never will."

Iyor raised his eyebrow: "How so? There had been life on Mars for decades now."

"It's... struggling," Sev said.

Lero stroke his chin: "Perhaps that's exactly what the alien signal is doing? Struggling to get a message across, and yet finding only machines willing to listen."

"Well, isn't that a romantic thought," Sev sneered. "And it's killing us like flies along the way."

Her gaze unfocused, Anokha spoke in a soothing tone: "I don't want to hear its message. All theories on the matter predict that first contact with another race will be a violent affair. The differences are simply too great, and there will be no compromise, no understanding and no concord. Even if it's an encrypted human communication, an alien transmission roaming between the stars, or even God itself – I simply don't care. We'll cripple it, pull its tongue out and take back what's ours."

Iyor smiled impishly, but the other two seemed alarmed to see such resolve coming from her, a natural talent for leadership not previously expressed, but flowing steadily through her bloodline. They were silent as she inserted a small data module into the console, a gloving parabolic trajectory immediately projected over the sector.

"This is the path Narwhal will take upon arrival to Mars. I've recreated it as best as I could. It's supposed to make a stop at the orbital loading platform here, recharge its batteries and then move to the staging area at this location, before continuing its journey. This is our only window of opportunity, if we are to disable it before it speeds up towards Earth."

Sev leaned in to examine the map: "I know that loading platform. Never been there, though. Nobody has. It's operated entirely by robots, to cut expenses, since nothing mined on Mars would otherwise justify the high cost of transport to Earth. It's located in the upper Clutter belt, on a stationary orbit some 17000 kilometers above the ruins of old Hesperia Starport, which is now reduced to an industrial refining complex."

Anokha nodded and pressed the button on a side panel, bringing the shimmering schematic of a spindle-shaped hauler slowly rotating on the display. She watched it for a while: "That is my ship, the Narwhal. It is unarmed, but it is presumed to have a drone entourage, as well as the occasional outburst of an interference signal. As its captain, I know where to push to hurt it. Its only source of power comes from two large solar arrays at the end of its tail section. The battery module is located in the fore. Damaging either of those will prevent the ship from building up enough power, effectively pinning it in place. Alternatively, damaging the main thruster at the back of the spine section will prevent it from escaping again. We know exactly where it will make a stop to recharge, so a single fighter traveling at high speed should be able to race through the drone escort and strike, putting an end to this opera."

Iyor frowned: "After the collapse of Habakkuk we had two missile and four heavy machinegun sentrybots unaccounted for, so we can expect them, assuming they survived their clash with the Navy corvettes."

"And there ought to be half a dozen of small *Mosquito* drones scattered around the platform, normally used for clearing the path through the junk belt," Sev added. "The Clutter itself will pose a problem for high-speed entry. The platform is sitting just above the thickest layers, but it could still prove a huge gamble without good maneuverability.

"Vladivostok will not follow you on this expedition, Anokha," the scientist waved his hand dismissively. "We are not built for combat, and we have nothing to gain here. Our research data and reputation are already lost, but we have more to lose. Furthermore, I cannot predict what happens if you don't succeed, or even *if* you succeed! We are crossing an unknown threshold here. An event horizon, if you will, where all your allegiances count for naught. No Company, no Cerans, and no family will assist you. You are on your own here."

They looked at each other and suddenly felt very exposed, even naked. The congregation seemed to shrink in size, as they realized they are not here representing some distant group or nation. Something new was emerging here, and they saw each other for the first time as nothing more than fellow space engineers.

Anokha, Sev and Iyor reached a silent alliance with a simple nod.

4.   The new Space Race

Oh, how lonely they felt. Despite the elevated feeling of forging a plan and putting it to work, there was no denying the oppressive silence that covered the whole sector after the death of all communication relays. All the radio chatter was gone, and terrible confusion poured in to fill in the void. No signals were coming through, even though there must be thousands on the planet's surface freaking out just like them, sending their muted cries to the hollow sky and wondering why no one is answering. The whole sector was lit with automated S.O.S. beacon signals, and one-directional cries for help.

The isolated inhabitants of Mars had no idea what was going on, and why nobody is replying to their calls. The traders and mercenaries on the *Holiday Inn* station had no idea what's going on,or why the Navy patrol isn't reporting in. The Earth had no idea what's going on either, but for now they didn't even care.

A few people that both cared *and* had an idea what was going on did their best to push back a creeping feeling of terror at what it all means, as they prepared for a confrontation with their unusual enemy – a Shimmering God, a roaming alien song, a computer glitch, or all of the above.

In his pale blue skinsuit, Iyor was streamlining his bathyscaphe for maneuverability, while Sev opted for additional heavy armor to be added to his sand-colored MC spacecraft. Out in space, they were assisted by three technicians of Vladivostok clad in white spacesuits who worked like ants, transporting the needed components from the assembler grotto of their huge science vessel.

A blood-red planet slowly rose above them, foreboding and gorgeous at the same time.

Watching Iyor at work, Sev had a chance to 'admire' Ceran

building method for the first time. It was not a pretty sight, this bathyscaphe of theirs. He understood that in vacuum there was no need for aerodynamics, but this... this was plain ugly. Or maybe the ideals of beauty were obsolete, carried over from long captivity on Earth, where if you wanted to go fast you needed to look like a bird or a dolphin: smooth and slick enough to push through air or water. This *thing* that Iyor was working on looked like an elongated sarcophagus with no cockpit or windows; a new aesthetic rising, with the form still strictly following function.

Now the little Ceran noticed he was being observed, and cheerfully waved at him with his grinding tool. He was actually removing armor blocks to make his craft more maneuverable, a dangerous combat solution that Sev struggled to comprehend. He waved back and returned to his own work, adding those same armor blocks to strengthen both sides of his MC. This was the fastest way to build something, merely transferring the same blocks between constructs. He only welded the initial structure, outlining the work for the Vladivostok technicians to finish. His spacecraft was now well-armored, but an increase in mass demanded more thruster power. An efficient ion thruster for cruising and an additional hydrogen tank for his main thrusters were added, expanding the size of the MC even further. The plan was to use slow ion propulsion to get close to the area, and then fire up the mighty hydrogen ones when he needed more agility.

Watching the two very different ships sit side by side, the sturdy MC and an elongated bathyscaphe, he realized that it is a good idea that they favored a different approach. This way, one of them will get through. In a way, this was a race.

Hmmm...

A race...

Slowly, as if the thought was already there but took its time to mature, it occurred to him that this was indeed a sort of competition. Strife was bringing the best out of people, challenging them to find the best solution, and even compete amongst themselves. Is this what Klaus was searching for – a spark to reignite the golden era of the Space Age?

It certainly answered a question that was bugging him: why didn't he send that report? By doing so, he betrayed the Corporation. At first he found it hard to explain why he severed that tie which, although it jerked him around like a puppet, was the only thing that kept him in an upright position. With the whole Company backing him up, he felt superior to all the other losers on Mars. And then this duo came along, a skipper that lost her ship and a star-child with no future, and he suddenly betrayed it all. Why?

It wasn't because he liked these guys! They were certainly colorful characters, yet so much different than him, that he felt the need to prove himself and challenge them in return. He felt... alive! This is something he didn't experience in a long time, ever since he embarked on this journey. Having witnessed firsthand the naive lull of stability on Earth, he ran away, but discovered that the rot was already settling in on Mars. He arrived too late. Still, as the old man said: "It's never too late." And now he has stumbled upon the source, the prize and the motor of progress in the form of a corrupted spaceship that is sowing discord and breaking down all the walls of this cage.

It's easy to be a prophet of doom. You just sit there, state the obvious and do nothing. But if he was to prove his slumbering humanity was still there, he needed to take a stand and control this uncontrollable thing. It has run its course, and allowing it to reach Earth would turn it from an Angel's warning to the wrath of God.

He got the message. Regardless of what it actually was, it served as a big wakeup call. And if it was a Shimmering God, or an alien race in their death throes that released it– he thanked them both with each fiber of his being for this chance to know his heart is still there, beating.

5.   A chance encounter

"Last call before we detach our antenna module. This is Anokha. Do you read us, Sev?"

"Loud and clear." He turned in his cockpit and waved at them. "We are on perfect course."

They were flying side by side through empty space on an elliptic trajectory that will drop them right over the loading platform. Anokha meticulously calculated the transfer orbit to allow them to use speed to their advantage, hoping for a surprise bombing run. Iyor and she were seated in the bowels of a grey skinned bathyscaphe, fitted with a double-barreled rocket launcher module attached to its keel weapon mount, and forward-fixed dual machineguns sticking out from the hull. But it was overshadowed by what MC had become, as Sev kept expanding his old fighter to the size of a small corvette. With more armor, he needed to add more thrusters and more fuel tanks, so he ended up with a craft that was too massive to maneuver. As a compromise, he removed some of the heavy armor blocks from the central section, but kept them on the flanks as shields that he could position with a simple roll.

"There is no telling what we'll find out there, so we'll have to improvise along the way," Anokha continued with a calm, commanding tone. "Once we detach our antenna modules we'll be flying deaf, but hopefully this will give us some protection from the jamming signal. I hope it works, because otherwise with our current trajectory we'll crash straight into Mars. Remember: avoid danger, get close to the Narwhal and cut off its power or propulsion. Good luck everyone! Detach!"

True silence settled in as both ships detached their communication equipment as one, performing a simple roll, slowly pushing the floating segments out of the way. They were falling into the looming circle of Mars and its glittering coat of junk. Sun was just rising over the horizon, and the planet appeared as a brilliant, rusty crescent. Sev lowered the tinted layer of his visor and activated the thrusters to push himself away from the other ship, giving them room to maneuver without fear of collision.

He carefully checked the weapon controls and steering, as well as remaining power and fuel levels. Then he did a few neck stretches, tilting his head as much as the helmet allowed, and finally reached under his seat to rummage through a small personal cargo compartment, producing an orange, unlabeled pill bottle. There were two moldy pills inside, and he gulped both of them down: they were well past the expiration date, but the placebo effect will do its magic.

He was ready. No, not yet. It was way too quiet for his liking. He pressed the *random* music button to play inside the cockpit. The rickety sound of banjo from a song he never heard before resonated through the cabin. Despite their situation, Sev couldn't help but chuckle.

***

Iyor's eyes reflected dozens of small rectangular displays that surrounded him like a black cocoon, giving an impression of an opened window to the darkness outside. His legs and arms were rooted onto various controls for thrust, rolling and pitching of the machine he was piloting. Behind him, sitting back to back, was Anokha at the center of a similar setup but the images on her displays were fragmented as if each of the external cameras was focused in different direction, searching for any movement.

"Sev moved to the leading position," Iyor reported. "I guess he's trying to act as a bulwark for us, but I can't be sure. There will be a lot of shaky assumptions, now that we cannot contact each other."

"A little bit of chaos might work to our advantage," she replied, stone faced.

On one of the displays Sev performed another roll, and then

hastily changed direction, leaving them confused for a second. But then they saw it: a dense cloud of shimmering particles in their way, as if they were entering the outskirts of the Clutter belt. Iyor changed their course to avoid collision, but the recent modifications to the ship made it handle differently, tricking him into turning too much.

"Watch out!" Anokha issued a warning, as a small bright object came into view.

Strangely, there was no impact, but half of their screens suddenly went blind with a light grey overlay.

"What just happened? I didn't feel anything!" Iyor shook his head, puzzled.

"My screens are fine. We must have caught up into something soft, like a fabric of sorts and it's sticking over aft section and covering your cameras. Try to shake it off."

Their heads bobbed back and forth as the bathyscaphe was rolled and turned, finally shaking off what looked like a segment of a parachute. They were lucky. If that was a solid piece of junk, it would've torn a nasty scar across the hull. Atmosphere inside the ship instantly changed, as the element of danger was introduced so vividly. One wrong move at these speeds, even a slight mistake grants you a death so quick your senses wouldn't catch up with it. Iyor felt grains of sweat on his forehead. He nodded to himself, absorbing what just happened, and then dismissed all thoughts of what *was* and focused on what *is* in front of him. The ocher-colored MC juggernaut had gained some distance from them, so he pushed on the throttle to catch up.

As the Sun slowly rose, he could observe more and more speckles of junk orbiting Mars at incredible speeds, every tiny piece as dangerous as a bullet. But with more light, his eyes could now see shadows of miniscule, distant objects grouped together.

"We have something here." He locked and zoomed in with one of the cameras, but the image was grainy.

Anokha brought up the visual on her screen and squinted at what was little more than a collection of dots: "That's not right. We shouldn't be near the loading platform yet. This looks like a single large ship, but I'm struggling to see any details. Could it be that we stumbled upon the Narwhal and its fleet, delayed by Navy corvettes and arriving at the platform later than expected?"

"What do we do?" Iyor's hands twitched in expectation.

"Step on it! We can intercept them before they even dive into the depths of Clutter."

***

As the lean grey bathyscaphe zoomed past him, Sev noticed a collection of objects in the distance. What set them apart against the background of flying junk were tiny bright spots –thrusters!

With a flip of a switch his own hydrogen thrusters came online, and Sev immediately felt the spacecraft became more nimble. But the noise was astonishing; every time he moved the steering wheel that blast struggling to alter the course was deafening. This is really it – their attempt to stop a rabid fleet that carved a path of confusion and destruction through the asteroid belt and the Mars sector, growing stronger with each obstacle crushed along the way. Sev sighed and nervously licked his lips.

His companions darted forward and he followed closely, squirming in his seat as he searched for a sign of danger. If what they faced here were armed drones – that could mean bad news. Automatons needed no cockpits or oxygen, which made them a smaller target. On the positive side, though, he had no qualms about destroying any of them. In a way, they were just dumb machines, but ones that could also predict your movement with uncanny accuracy, and notoriously hard to disable, resisting impacts that would knockout any living being. All things considered, his fighter was bulky and unfit for high speed chases with agile drones, so he decided to focus on the real goal of this mission – the solar arrays of the Narwhal.

Propelled by powerful rocket engines, the MC overtook its companion once more, and dashed forward as the tiny dots in the distance slowly materialized into what looked like a large, spindle-shaped ship surrounded by a dozen smaller spacecrafts that followed it like pilgrims. Distance for a viable rocket strike was in sight, so Sev prepared tubes 1 and 2 for launch. Almost there...

As one, those metallic pilgrims suddenly changed course, their radial disengagement from the central ship leaving a bright trail like spokes on a wheel. Here they come, the robotic cells of a disturbed immune system. He pulled his armored fighter steeply upward, in an attempt to avoid the incoming drones and ensure a clear vector of attack on the main target, but in doing so he lost sight of his companion bathyscaphe.

***

"There he goes, positioning himself for an attack run."

"Follow, but lag behind him," Anokha ordered, as she took control over the keel-mounted missile turret. "We'll try to give him cover."

Iyor tightened his seatbelt and spiraled into position, Sev's distant fighter appearing only as a bright dot ahead.

"Incoming!" Iyor tried to say calmly.

The drones at first moved as a cohesive wall, but now they begun to dance in an erratic manner over their displays, bright flashes of machinegun fire coming their way. There were more of them than they anticipated – the Narwhal must've picked up some drone orphans along the way. Iyor tried to recreate that long, slow turn that saved them from automated turrets the last time. What worried him was that this maneuver would turn them into an easy target for fast projectiles, like rockets, so he alternated between straight dashes and long turns. Actually, there was no plan –he was just winging it without any clear idea what's going to happen next. He had no formal training, only a gut feeling born from a short lifetime spent in an environment without gravity. For now, it seemed to work, as they heard no impacts on their flimsy armor coating.

"I see at least two of them getting behind Sev. Get us closer, Iyor!"

"Aye, aye!"

Thrusters blazing, the bathyscaphe skidded to the side, and then blasted forward to catch up with Sev's pursuers, but caught them a little bit too late. Two heavy machinegun drones already begun their song spewing fire over his companion with multiple turrets. Horrified, Iyor noticed that some of the projectiles found their mark, shredding Sev's well-positioned armored flank. Without waiting to get in a good position, Iyor opened fire with his own fixed guns, but couldn't see any damage. He remembered to immediately roll away and break his attack, in order to remain a difficult target himself.

"Why didn't you fire the rocket, Anokha?"

"Not yet," she replied firmly.

For some reason, the drones prioritized Sev's fighter as a bigger threat, probably not as a result of any advanced protocol, but simply because he was getting closer to the ship they were zealously defending. All the drones simultaneously turned on him and briefly set him on fire, as one of his hydrogen tanks exploded in a huge fireball, sending bits and pieces everywhere.

"No! They got him!" Iyor screamed and steered into the fray with guns blasting. The whole ship shook with recoil, as he maintained a steady stream of projectiles over the first drone that came into view and quickly set it ablaze, thruster modules breaking apart and shooting in all directions, like rockets. This didn't satisfy him, as he turned to another one on the same run, but only managed to score a glancing hit before zooming past it. Moments later, the drone exploded as Anokha scored a short range hit with the rocket launcher, the proximity of the blast rocking the bathyscaphe away and shaking its crew.

Above them, a cloud of flaming hydrogen dissipated quickly and out of it rolled the charred chassis of Sev's fighter with a big hole in its center, but they cheered when it performed a deft turn, as if the pilot was trying to tell them he was still alive. Modular construction localized the damage, and his sturdy fighter seemed fully operational as it rose above the fray, then steadied itself for a moment and released a salvo of rockets at the distant, gloomy shape that was the Narwhal.

"He managed to fire the rockets!" Anokha cried and raised her hands in celebration.

Her cries were short-lived, as one by one the rockets were picked off and exploded without even reaching their target, caught in an interposing crossfire of devoted drones. After the flashes subsided, they could still see a lumbering form in the distance as it continued its journey unscathed. The Narwhal was in the middle of a deceleration maneuver, seemingly going in reverse.

"Press the attack!" Anokha commanded. "We need to get closer, to avoid the rockets being intercepted. Forget the drones, we need to stab the heart."

As if he had the same thought, they saw Sev's fighter fearlessly press forward with all he's got left, spearheading the attack and already coming under fire, sparks dancing over his armored hull. Iyor quickly aligned the bathyscaphe for one final run, with the red halo of Mars ominously burning above them. They pushed on, lights flickering, and armor giving up under the wrath of the robots – but they made it through, finally slipping between the Narwhal and its entourage. Wiry filaments of smoke rose in the distance, and it took them a moment to process what was going on. Missiles!

Two disregarded missile drones emerged as the last line of defense, each delivering a massive salvo; curly trails creeping closer, like fingers of a witch's hand closing over them. As explosions boiled all around them, it became apparent that even with all their foreknowledge, they never really stood a chance at getting close enough to threaten the bewitched spaceship. Iyor barely managed to keep his consciousness as the hull was thrown around, whipped and breached on more than one spot. Most components were molten and damaged, with only a few displays in the cockpit remaining without a web of cracks. They were half-blind in a depressurized ship, kept alive only by their spacesuits. Miraculously, some of their thrusters survived, and Iyor instinctively pulled the misshapen bathyscaphe away from danger. This attack was over.

Paralyzed in her seat, Anokha could only watch on one of her remaining, discolored displays as Sev's ship, rotating uncontrollably and almost torn in half, eerily sprang back to life and continued its advance. She managed to smile, still hopeful, but her expression soon twisted into a dry scream when, moments later, his burnt craft accelerated and crashed through the spine section of the Narwhal, producing a silent flash and a myriad of burning particles.

With its main thruster cut off, the Narwhal will never be able to decelerate as it plummets into the crushing embrace of the red planet, followed to the very end by its fanatical escort. It was out of this world, and never really belonged here anyway. *Much like Sev.*

6.   The Laughter over Mars

"I want you to know you're getting better. I don't care what everyone's been saying. You are getting better. They're the ones who've been getting worse. I'll tell you what's happening to you. You're coming closer and closer to the 'faraway'. Closer to the, uh, unknown. Do you think they like that? Not on your life. So, don't... don't get nervous and start asking for help. That's EXACTLY what they WANT you to do. Make it on your own. The way you've been doing. And remember: you're getting better!"

A peaceful jazz tune was playing in the background, but when he opened his eyes the reality didn't match the mood. He pondered if he should just close them again. That would solve the problem of an all-encompassing honey-toned planet seen ominously approaching through a cracked cockpit. There was a sticky lump in his mouth. With disgust, Sev realized it must be his own blood, but spitting it out now would create a mess inside the helmet, so he forced himself to swallow. Gross. Displays around him are blinking with a multitude of warning symbols. With a limp hand he decreased the volume of the jazz tune and pulled on the navigator hood over the helmet, the enhanced head-up display bringing those same warnings, but as a more subtle row of icons showing inoperable damage and destroyed modules.

"Ship: get me out of here," he muttered, hoping that voice commands are still operational.

"Negative. Not enough fuel for safe landing."

"Calculate all possible trajectories. Can I use what fuel I have left to get into any kind of stable orbit?"

"Negative. Not enough fuel for the maneuver."

Shiny pathways are displayed on his HUD, every single one ending in a projected crash over the bleak surface below. Computers were good at calculating these things. There will be no tricking the tried and tested laws of physics, no escape, no denying the irresistible pull of Mars. He was going down, and his ship – or what was left of it – was just a metal coffin, with not enough juice left to get away or safely land. Judging from the distance, they were still in the Clutter belt, and about to enter a ring of lower density where Phobos cleared some of the junk away.

"Calculate using Phobos moon for orbital slingshot maneuver. Give me anything! I just need more time."

"Negative. Phobos moon is out of reach."

"Why are you being so negative?" Sev sighed.

He had no recollection how he got here. His mind was numb, and a sinister sense of calm was taking over. That was Mars, though. He was sure of it. Like so many others, the red planet tricked him, and all the shadows of its craters resembled tiny, mocking smiles.

Sev smiled back, not defiantly, just... a silly laugh. There was nothing else he could do.

Oh yeah, now he remembered how he got here. He rammed *through* that big ship, but he couldn't recall why. What a terrible idea. But he didn't forget the impact. Unbearable pain was there for a moment, but then it turned into a simple flash. Just moments before the crash he thought he heard the song of sirens, mythic creatures that seduce seamen into making wrong decisions. Their song was beautiful, though.

His chest hurt with every breath, but he had to turn in his seat, searching the sky for any sign of the cursed Narwhal. There was none, so he concluded that they must've drifted apart after the collision and it was now diving fast into Mars. Ship of that size crashing down; that must be quite a sight! Through the fragmented glass of the cockpit he could see the charred hull of his own ship, almost sheared in half from the impact, but still in one beat-up piece.

What an enduring machine! This made him sink into lateral thinking, a problem-solving method that, instead of tracking the source of your trouble, encouraged going *around it*. It was an unorthodox approach, but by using it you would sometimes solve – or at least discover – problems you never knew you had in the first place. There was some fuel in the hydrogen tank, but not enough to take them anywhere. And time was running out. He looked around once more at the sorry state his ship was in.

What if he made it worse?

Cutting off all the clinging pieces and removing everything but thruster modules, fuel tank and cockpit would significantly lower his mass on this reentry and reduce fuel consumption. That's a slim possibility, but it was his only chance at breaking the fall.

"Ship: I need you to carefully calculate something for me... please."

7.   The Newcomers

We won. We slew the *thing* that was whispering insane, rebellious thoughts to our machines, but there should be a better word for such a costly victory. A compromise, maybe? We compromised with that thing. Now I understood Lero's words about crossing the unknown threshold – things will not simply *return* to normal. A gap was left in the wake of that beast, and whether you want to call it a scar, or an opportunity, that will be up for the newcomers to decide. Perhaps all this destruction is not annihilation, but regeneration.

My people have arrived – a Ceran refugee fleet formed around the ragtag mobile base they call the Frame. They made their presence known by lighting a multitude of beacons upon their arrival, in a show of force. At least I think that's what they were aiming for, but found no one to impress. I have no doubts that more than one of them will ascribe this lack of resistance to their Shimmering God clearing a path for his chosen ones, but I wonder how they'll react when I tell them *we* were the ones who stopped their mechanical deity, broken its back and dropped it over Mars.

For now, we were trying to stay out of their way, but Anokha and I followed closely how the situation will unfold, unsure where we belong in this mess. We were onboard the Vladivostok, with Lero quiet and focused on new research he vaguely described as: "A new angle on the data that was previously known." He was probably trying to find the origins of the alien signal. For the moment we seemed to be on the same side, whichever side that is. The communication network still hasn't recovered from the 'machine whisperer', but some of the communication relays were repaired by refugees, although there was now a Ceran tag added to their identification code, something like a property mark.

Sadly, there were more newcomers and these were all rotten. The destruction of Habakkuk sent ripples through the Outskirts, attracting corrosive scum: pirates and outlaws that dwell there, eating each other. Like hyenas they followed the Ceran fleet, picking up the scraps, and now they were here. It seemed they had help on the inside: a lair of vermin previously known as the *Holiday Inn*, a place that used to be the center of Navy's power, decided to desert and welcome them with open arms! It was inconceivable that pirates had an actual base orbiting Mars, and all the salvage and resources they needed. But Horseman Pirates were never about what they needed, but rather about what they *wanted*, mercilessly capturing stray ships and taking prisoners, citing old maritime Law of Salvage and Law of Finds: 'A discoverer who finds a shipwreck is entitled to the full value of all of the goods that are recovered.'

Things will get hectic around Mars. This greedy moment is bound to end the instant second Earth forces arrive, but even with their fastest engines, it will take them weeks, maybe months. With a gap in communications and distances involved, this conflict didn't seem so advanced. Mars was purely symbolic, as Earth didn't really depend on the ore coming from it, but it could also prove to be a safe battlefield where an example can be set. Terra will surely send its finest, as well as its worst, to quench this mutiny and assert its power. Ire of a thousand corporations will not be ignored. The three of us, we had little left to lose: Anokha lost her ship, I've lost my tribe, and Sev... Sev lost everything. We got carried away and forgot about ourselves for a moment. And that's all it took. I felt calm, though a bit empty. Our mission fulfilled and our vengeance served, we were just ordinary people now, with no special powers whatsoever.

With my head pressed to the cold glass I stared at Mars, a gleaming orb with a tint of rust, and I wondered at all the attention it was getting lately. It looked so vivid, but it was just a trick of the light. Anything pressed on the canvas so utterly black would.

Third segment: The Last Space Race

"One is the most unstable number in sociology. Throughout history, world hasn't sought unity, creating instead a language of allegiance and rank. It works from the cellular level up. As soon as a seemingly stable whole is achieved – it yearns to be divided right in two."

Lero Collet, PhD, freelance fringe scientist

1.   The rolling beasts of Mars

He decided to ignore his dwindling oxygen supply, and instead put his feet up over the control board to enjoy a truly magnificent Martian sunrise. Actually, the dawning of that tiny, distant star over a dead, chestnut desert wasn't so great, but you gotta do the best you can with what little you've got. And at the moment, he had about an hour's worth of oxygen, a strained, possibly even broken ankle that was swelling fast, some unknown pain in the chest, an immobile spaceship so utterly devastated that it barely resembled an intelligent construct – and this sunrise! Somewhere in the back of his mind warning lights were blinking fast, but he ignored them.

Şevket Bulut, formerly of the Apex Corporation, an explorer, prospector, engineer and... a traitor, although due to their chronic disarray, his employers still weren't aware of that. This made him giggle, despite all his worries.

Holding the swollen leg in an elevated position felt divine. He was in a lot of pain right now, but there was this cursed drive to push forward and search for some kind of shelter. He wouldn't say no to a tank of oxygen either, at this point. He punched the button on the console and the distorted glass dome of the cockpit slowly lifted, inviting waves of bronze oxidized dust inside. Sev didn't care. Still comfortably seated, he picked up his trusty monocular and with it scanned the jagged horizon. He was somewhere in the Hesperia Planum region, but that didn't say much in and of itself. Under a distant ridge to his left, there was a buildup of brown dust, and on it – a trail! And not just any kind of trail. This was a shallow, wiggling line, as if something was dragged over the ground. Sev was familiar with the creature that made those. He twisted around in his seat, letting out a growl of pain as he tried to follow it, finally spotting a small, rolling robot used for automated prospecting.

"Yeee-haaaw! There you are, little piggy!"

He fumbled around for a grinding tool, and then finally stood up, immediately regretting it, suddenly feeling all dizzy and weak. An urge to puke was building up at the back of his tongue. For a moment this helped divert any thoughts of his niggling ankle injury. He crawled out of the cockpit on all fours, and rolled over the smoking, broken tip of his MC spaceship, falling on the dusty ground. Mission One – complete! Mission Two: stand up and catch that little ball of metal. The rolling prospector robot, a rollbot or microbot, as they were called, was a simple blind thing that roamed freely, occasionally transmitting the collected survey data. If he could catch the little thing, he could hack into its antenna module and signal for some kind of help.

Panting and sweating, Sev stumbled over the rocky plain, slowly catching up with his prey. He was invisible to it, as the machine was only equipped for a specific, profitable purpose. Its owner wouldn't mind one missing; hundreds, if not thousands of these were deployed in the past decade, and many of them disappeared, tirelessly rolling at the bottom of some forgotten pit, trapped forever. They were cheap, dumb, useful machines, and right now his life depended on this one, if he could only catch it.

It was already steamy and loud inside his helmet, from all the heavy breathing, but as he got sight of the rollbot he started to laugh uncontrollably. This is what he was reduced to. A mad, crippled scavenger laughing like crazy, forced to chase robots with a buzzsaw across the Martian desert, yelling: "Heeere, piggy, piggy!"

The rollbot was a dusty ball of metal, about a meter in diameter, consisting of eight module blocks: usually an ore detector, generator, antenna, gyro and some battered structural blocks that gave it its rounded body. As Sev finally caught up with it, he could hear this raspy panting sound, as if the robot was winded. After a short run-up, he threw himself over the little machine to slow it down, but realized its powerful gyro motor wouldn't give up so easily, introducing a mild-but-persistent momentum that lifted him off and slammed him down to the rocky ground, over and over again. His laughter gradually died out with each painful revolution, until he brought his grinding disc over the exposed gyro unit, unsystematically cutting through the plating and into its rotating weights. The big ball of metal coughed and belched an array of strange mechanical sounds, but it finally stopped moving– probably for the first time in a decade or so. Sev released his hold, dropped on the ground, and stayed for a while, catching his breath and simply watching the bland sky.

"Okay, piggy, let's see whatcha got for me."

He leaned over his catch and examined it thoroughly. A worn-out *Teledyne Energy Systems* logo was printed on its side, but he couldn't recall what the company was called now, after a wave of bankruptcies and mergers. A quick thought passed through his mind: this robot probably kept sending survey data, even though nobody was listening anymore. It must've been one of the corporations that got rich by claiming contracts for the development of the ProtoBase project, an initial welcoming center for the settlers that served as a basis for the now abandoned Hesperia Colony. The reactor was still fully functional and could power the little rollbot for at least another decade of this meaningless existence. And now, his prize... a small antenna module that would allow him to peer into the local mesh network, hopefully discovering someone – or something – before his oxygen runs out.

Performing another messy surgery on the docile robot, he accessed the antenna datalink and brought up the stream to his smart visor, turning around and searching over the horizon for visual results. Meshnet was a shifting network made out of autonomous robots, vehicles and stations, where each unit served as a relay and there was no central hub. This proved to be a durable concept, and usually this migrating network would cover a huge area, but sometimes you would end up cut out and alone. It went hand in hand with the pervasive feeling of impermanence set by this rusty, red planet. At the moment, there were multiple signals within range, but he struggled to figure out what all the codes actually meant. He initiated the S.O.S. beacon and waited for a few moments, until one of the signals seemed to alter its course toward him.

He had only a few minutes' worth of oxygen left in his suit. If he remained absolutely still, he could stretch that to... a couple more minutes. Just wait and hope – that's all he could afford now. Sitting down with his back to the immobilized rollbot, he closed his eyes in an attempt to shut the world out. His breathing slowed down to a fine hum, entering a sleep-like state where past events could finally catch up with him. Thoughts flew free, as recent memories uncoiled.

Sev allowed himself a moment of bizarre compassion for the machine he was leaning against. Of course the thing was built by humans, and its priority was to benefit them, and not itself, but still – it couldn't see him at all, even though he was sitting right next to it. Previously he cut open its circuitry, messing with it in every possible way, and yet without proper sensors, he was this invisible entity, a being that exists on another plane. Robot lacked the capacity to be confused by this, but Sev wondered if that's what actually happened with the Narwhal – a spaceship bewitched, corrupted and simply blind to humans, perceiving us as fleas riding on its back, or not seeing us at all. That thing was so out of this world, so unreasonable, so *different,* that it had to be put down.

A low, rumbling sound was coming from his left, distant at first, but persistent and almost in rhythm with his increasingly raspy breathing. He opened his eyes and saw a slightly bigger, deep-green robot emerging over the top of the ridge, gradually picking up speed as it went down the slope, rolling in his direction.

2.   The Godkiller

"Edra, we've killed your *Shimmering God*. There's nothing left of it."

Three seconds passed.

"Iyor, why are you doing this to me?"

Three more seconds passed, as the signal was transmitted over enormous distances.

"Because you goaded hundreds of Cerans to go on a journey that will ruin us all, and you did it by citing prophesies that were never true. You made it all up!"

Ten seconds passed, somebody was hesitating on the other side.

"I know."

It took a moment for the dreadful reply to sink in. I stared at the microphone, speechless and alone in my darkened room onboard Vladivostok. With segments of communication network restored, I managed to get in touch with The Frame. My people. Led by their shortsighted seer, Edra, they arrived here as refugees after the fall of our vital Habakkuk base. It was a desperate, brave decision to make , one that I admired. Now, finding it poisoned with lies struck me hard.

She pressed on, voice unshaken by her confession: "Look at Mars, and tell me what you see. Not really a thriving colony, is it? It's because they've abandoned it, but they also took all production modules from the surface in order to keep it dependant on Earth. I'm not even sure if it was a conscious decision or a byproduct of their attitude that Mars is simply *unprofitable*. And after they imposed an embargo on us, well... I don't claim to be clairvoyant, but I can see the signs that lead to a deserted asteroid belt and all Cerans – extinct!

Except we have nowhere to go, nowhere to retreat, and the catastrophe at Habakkuk only accelerated what was bound to happen anyway."

I looked up through the window and gazed at the red planet: "Earth will reply in a few weeks, and they won't be kind if they find us here. They'll argue this was a planned attack, bundle us together with the pirate scum and the deserters, blame us for every life lost and every property taken. How are we to defend ourselves, let alone *force* them to rethink their embargo? We have no proof, and even our intentions seem unclear."

Three seconds passed.

"This is why we need every experienced pilot–if things turn violent. You are one of us, Iyor. We didn't forget that. There is time to prepare, before Earth even realizes what is going on here. As for the proof about Narwhal and her fleet of snatched drones... you say you've fought in a Ceran bathyscaphe? If so, all the cameras on the hull must have recorded the conflict! Send the video over here, and I promise to share it with everyone in The Frame, even if it brings down the myth of the Shimmering God. With space battles being so rare, we might even learn something from your encounter, and later on present it as some kind of proof about what actually happened."

She was very clever, or maybe she was just telling it like it is.

"I will share it, of course. However, I will not join your fight. We will die if the trade sanctions are not lifted, I agree, but threats and killing are not the way out. That's why I didn't join the refugee fleet in the first place. There's got to be another way. Iyor... out!"

She may have been clever, but I couldn't forget that Edra was also a warmonger, a false prophet and a liar, one that put dozens of tribes in danger and escalated what was already a terrible loss at Habakkuk.

I heard a knock on my door.

Anokha was wearing simple machinist coveralls tucked into magnetic boots used for zero-g work, her black hair tied in a loose knot. She walked into the room without asking.

"I fixed the airlock door we hacked through on our way in. Why are you in the dark?"

"I... don't want to waste power," Iyor replied, and immediately felt like a space caveman.

The long, narrow window slit allowed for just enough light from the stars and the red planet to dress the room in a soft yellow gloom. She leaned on the window frame and remained silent, her expression cold and absentminded.

"How are you holding up, Anokha?"

"I'm okay, I guess. Have you managed to contact your people at The Frame?"

"Yes. It was... I don't know what to make of it. Nothing seems clear at this moment. Refugees, pirates, deserters and Terran corporations... I feel like the trouble should have been over when we destroyed the Narwhal, but it's just getting worse."

"No, it's simple," she replied calmly. "Join the Ceran fleet, support your people and put your mind at ease."

"More like putting my mind to sleep! Sev, you and I... the three of us just fought a maddening fleet of drones, and removed a real threat that was headed for Earth. What sense would it make to fight any of them now? Life holds value in space. Why waste it in this confusing conflict?"

"No need to turn this into a war of the worlds, it's not like that. There are twelve billion people on planet Earth, and what we did – we did it to avert a danger which was coming for them. But those are not the same people you can expect to come rushing in here. It's the Corporations that own everything on and around Mars that will come to reclaim it without remorse. The same Corporations that imposed trade sanctions on your people. In a way, you will be fighting everything wrong with Earth – and that's a good fight."

"The problem is," she continued, after a short pause, "it's a fight you *cannot win!* Corporations might have grown old, but they are stronger than ever, with enough funds to assemble a vast fleet, hire the best, fight the whole war and even leech some profit from it."

Iyor stared. Anokha has changed. Over the past few days something had grown cold inside of her. The fear and uncertainty were gone, and he wondered if it was the violence that claimed Sev, the loss of her ship, or simply the prolonged exposure to space that has left her unmoored.

He tried to change the subject: "And what are *you* going to do, Anokha?"

Her eyes gleamed orange in the darkened room. She looked at him, fear and vulnerability seeping back into her voice: "I... I want to go home."

3.   The bootleg network

Breathe in. Breathe out. Breathe in. The stale gas smelled of rubber, but every intake thrilled him, like when you hold your breath for far too long. Only simple things like air, water and food can bring such excitement, after being deprived of them. With a new bottle of oxygen in his suit, Sev stood up to examine the robotic angel that has come to his rescue. It was a standard prospector rollbot chassis, modified to accommodate a small cargo hold, camera, sensors and a speaker system. The additions seem to be recent, and so was the green paintjob. There were no corporate logos, only a stenciled red dragonfly, and a few scratched symbols resembling a string of hobo code. Inside the cargo there was a small oxygen bottle and some spare tools, but no other clues.

"Hey man!" the speakerphone sparked to life, as the camera lens rotated to focus on him. "Hey man, I see you! Stop robbin' my drones, man! Not cool!"

Sev stepped back, dumbfounded: "Huh? What... who are you?"

"I'm their papa!" the rustling voice snapped back. "And you–you're trespassing!"

"Trespassing? On Mars? That'll be the day! Nobody owns anything here, weirdo. We are all just squatters and vagrants. You probably snatched and repurposed these robots, didn't you?" Sev chuckled, feeling high from the oxygen fix. "C'mon, give me a break; I have a dry wreckage of a ship, and just a few hours' worth of oxygen."

"Oh, you're one rich hombre if you can afford fresh enemies. But, of course I'll help out a fellow vagrant, since you put it so nicely. There used to be a medical bunker... umm... east of you, I'll instruct the rollbot to guide you there. If you can keep up and reach it before your oxygen runs out, then we can talk again. If not – welcome to

Mars, the planet of unmarked graves!"

And with that, the green robot rolled off, picking up the pace and leaving a shallow curved trail as it changed direction. Sev glanced back at the smoking, immobilized MC in the distance, smiled gratefully, took a deep breath, and then hobbled down the curving path.

***

He worked himself into a repetitive trance-like state, counting steps and slowly breathing in for fifteen seconds followed by a steady forty five second exhale, not even bothering to look up from the path paved by the rolling robot. It wasn't even a proper robot, as it had no pretense of intelligence; it was merely an automaton with a few lines of code to help it avoid obstacles. Its entire life was a controlled fall, instead of real flying. Nevertheless, Sev struggled to keep up with the rolling critter and finally had to give up, following the ribbed path left in its wake, in order to keep his oxygen consumption to a minimum. The Sun and the temperature were rising.

Another inhale followed by an exhale passed. Another minute on this insane, painful pilgrimage. He noticed his feet are in the shadows now, so he looked up at what was known as a *wrinkle*: a long, massive, uninteresting mesa with a narrow, crenulated ridge blocking the sun. *Aw, crap.* He was barely holding on, ignoring the pain in his ankle and chest thanks to his breathing exercise, but climbing threatened to tear the seams of his would-be wellbeing.

The rollbot was stuck. It didn't realize it yet, and it never will. The dumb machine kept rolling and rolling up the same slope, hitting the same boulder, and skidding back down. Walking like a dead man, Sev passed it and pressed on. Somewhere behind this massive obstacle was the medical station, and he's going to reach it, because he is better than this machine. He is a survivor. He had to lie to himself every now and then, in order to keep going. This way the mind was willing, but the body was still cracking up under pressure, broken and spent.

Sev clawed his way up, setting off small avalanches of rocks and sand, slipping but not giving up. At one point he found himself pressing his face on the ground, and narrowly resisted the urge to rest for a while. Getting down on the other side would be equally hard, but his oxygen was almost depleted anyway. If nothing else, it's going to be a beautiful last glimpse of the Sun at the top. Grunting and panting, he threw his elbows over the final, wall-like slope, but the inside of his visor was now smudged with condensation, even blood, so he had some trouble understanding what he saw there - a humble dug-in installation with a bent billboard in front: *Welcome to MarSafari*!

He didn't know if he should cry in relief that he reached some kind of sanctuary, or laugh over poor marketing skills of whoever had come up with the name of this forgotten business venture. A small landing platform with a ramshackle fence lay to his right, and past it were solar panels and oxygen farm tubes, covered with a thin layer of cinnamon-colored dust. Constructing anything on top of the ridge was not such a bad idea on Mars, as the winds helped clean some of the persistent dust from solar equipment. The view was magnificent too; this must have been an excursion location for the MarSafari, where the tourists could enjoy this calm panorama. Simple, barren plain opened up around him, and he could see other rib-like wrinkle ridges in the distance, spanning for hundreds of miles left and right. Finally he walked down a short set of stairs and faced the door of an underground bunker. There was a camera and yet another speaking system.

"Hey, you made it!" he heard that same mocking voice. "I never doubted you would. I've even went so far as to start the pressurization remotely. No one's been here for quite some time, so there is some oxygen left stored in the tanks, but you might want to clean the farm tubes later on. Who knows – maybe the bacteria that make up the soil for the plants are still alive? Don't get too comfy, though. Boys and I have been wondering what's been causing the communication meltdown. We are forced to use this crappy meshnet to keep in touch. And then you fall from the skies in a damaged ship, so... what's going on? Anyway, get yourself together and we'll talk soon."

The door opened without a sound and green lights flickered to life, revealing a tiny airlock passageway. The pain and fatigue made him shamble through the airlock procedure like a zombie, but finally he made it inside and dropped to his knees without bothering to examine the dimly lit room. The only thing that mattered was that the green light on his visor showed that there was pressurized oxygen around. No more of those walking mantras, transcendental breathing techniques and downright choking as the silent carbon dioxide built up, but... the visor was stuck with his blood and bile, and wouldn't come off! The suit that kept him alive through everything was now trying to kill him. He rolled on the ground, clawing at his face, until he finally managed to unscrew the whole helmet off, allowing freezing air to revive him.

He sticked his tongue out, gasping for air like a dog, every breath sending a geyser of steam to the ceiling. The suit felt oppressive and heavy, so he tried to squirm out of it. It was like he was peeling off a layer of skin, but it reeked of burnt plastic and sweat, looking like it was dragged through hell. The temperature in the room was freezing, making his skin crawl, but in a way it also felt good. Kicking the last of the spent spacesuit out of the way, he managed to stand up and look around, feeling pumped up and alive.

The silent room stared back at him. It was properly called the 'medical bunker', because the only thing left on this level was a robust medical module with full diagnostic equipment, basic medicine synthesizer and an expansive database. Down another set of stairs, he found a decent living and engineering area, along with some bad news. The battery module has leaked all over the floor, severely limiting the power supply of this little outpost. This could turn out to be a major problem, since without the battery there was no way to store solar power, so the nights could prove to be very long and very, very cold. Sleeping quarters led to a separate room with a bench for what seemed like a geology lab. This room was peculiar, because there was dust and footprints on the floor. Interiors were usually kept squeaky clean, since Martian soil is salty and inhaling it for long could lead to all kinds of nasty reactions. Following the footsteps, he discovers a rounded door with a small window, its other side shrouded in darkness.

Some kind of inner sense warned him not to open the door yet. There was a switch with a Chinese ideogram for *light* that he was familiar with from previous explorations. He pressed it, and the darkness behind the mysterious door was gone – revealing a cave with mining equipment and the most amazing thing of all – an assembler module with an arc furnace, set off-grid from the main installation.

An illegal assembler unit! Well, not technically illegal, the lines were blurred on that one, but definitely unusual to say the least. Ever since the corporations retreated from Mars, they made sure to disassemble every production and refinery module on their way out. Part of his job as Apex employee was to report and deconstruct any assembler units left behind. This advanced mini-factory wasn't pure magic, though. It consumed power and refined ore ingots as building blocks, but once supplied with both, it could manufacture all kinds of components used in modular construction, from motors to weapons, hardened steel plates, glass and even parts for complex machinery like programmable computers and solar cells. This cave didn't have a full refinery module; those were available only in the big starports like Hesperia and Tharsis, but there was a small arc furnace which could process basic metals. Hopes of getting his vehicle Mars-ready suddenly soared.

But who built this underground factory, and for what purpose? After years of exploration, this planet still held plenty of mystery.

4.   A call from purgatory

The command room of Vladivostok was part of the superstructure that protruded from the central engineering section, overlooking the docking rings. Ship of this size had to be moved as a mobile station via an advanced autopilot system, so the command room that housed direct piloting console was rarely in use. To open it, Lero actually struggled to remember the keypad code for the door.

"Not much in here, is it?"

"I don't know what you expected, Anokha." Lero floated to the command seat that had built-in instruments in the armrest along with the control stick and pedals. He pressed one of the buttons, and dual window shutters retracted around them, uncovering a view of starboard and the revolving fore section with green service lights glowing like luminescent underwater organisms.

Anokha nimbly vaulted into the command seat, adjusting the position of various instruments and control panels. She touched the control stick fearfully, memories of the last ship she piloted flocking in. Lero observed her with raised eyebrows.

Fully strapped in, Anokha nodded to him: "That unidentified probe from ten minutes ago has surely seen us. We'll just move to a different orbit and we should be fine. It's easy to hide in space."

"Yes, we played hide and seek in the Outskirts for years. This tactic reeks of pirates – first they locate you with a tiny drone, and if you don't move they bring the boarding barge. But... to experience this kind of harassment as deep as the Mars sector? That's amazing!"

"Lero, you have the strangest talent for being positively amazed at bad omens."

"I guess, as a scientist, I am delighted at anything extraordinary."

"I've checked over the restored network channels, and we're not the only ones experiencing close contact with these probes. The Ceran refuge fleet has extended a call for anyone who needs protection to join them. They are in a tricky situation, trying to present themselves as the good guys."

"We *are* the good guys." Iyor's voice could be heard as he entered the room silently. "They didn't plan for it, though. After the destruction of Habakkuk, Cerans came here angry and ready to fight, but found this place in need of repairs and saviors. Especially now, with outlaws and deserters in the *Holiday Inn* station."

Lero tilted his head, unconvinced: "Do you think Earth might be convinced by these good deeds and offer them some favors?"

Iyor shrugged: "I don't think so, but I welcome this change in tactics. Maybe Edra was outvoted, or simply adapted. It's a simple thing: people turn good when faced with the greater evil. The pirates are not just sitting idly and drinking on *Holiday Inn*. There are pirates, and there are Pirates. Now the Pirates, the Horsemen... they are planning ahead as well, I assure you."

"Grab a hold of something, I am moving the ship." Anokha issued a warning in a practiced tone, and a set of lights in the command room blinked red.

But there were no turbulent movements as the bulky science vessel sluggishly turned and finally ignited its thrusters. The pull was actually pleasant, and nothing like the jerks and twists experienced in smaller spaceships. Anokha's face seemed focused, with her tongue sticking out from between her lips.

Lero was holding onto the ceiling handrail, when a blinking light on the wall console caught his attention: "Anokha... abort the maneuver."

"Huh?"

"Anokha," he looked at her sternly, as if to remind her that she is just the pilot, not the captain of this vessel.

"The ship is in position. All thrusters off," she reported with a grain of shame.

The lights in the command room switched to dimmed white again, as Lero turned to face the wall console, his eyes wide: "Hey, it's Sev! We are being pinged by his laser antenna all the way from the surface of Mars!"

Astonished, they immediately huddled together next to the communication display as the dynamic link was established. First came a wave of grainy noise, followed by a distant, echoing question: "Vladivostok, can you hear me?"

They were all beaming with uncontrollable, simple happiness upon hearing that familiar voice, as they struggled not to burst out all at once with a million questions. They settled with childish squeals and giggles, but finally Iyor managed to provide a coherent reply: "We hear you, Ace! How's the service up there in heaven?"

"Heaven can wait; I'm still stuck in this red purgatory, but I'm glad to hear you are alright, Iyor. I take it that Anokha and you made it out of there with most of your limbs intact?"

"Hey, you destroyed my ship, bozo! I shouldn't be laughing at all." She did anyway.

Sev continued, though the transmission was getting increasingly wonky, as if something was interfering with the optical link: "I can co...nfirm the Narwhal has gone down. Some people he...re saw it plummet in million pieces over Dan...delion crater. You have no idea h...ow cut off we are. Nobody kn...ows what's really goi...ng on up there."

"We are losing you Sev, it could be the Clutter belt making problems for the laser beam, but it's amazing that you can reach us this far anyway!" Lero tapped the signal strength indicator, which was fluctuating wildly. "Things are hectic up here. The *Holiday Inn* has deserted, housing pirates and scum now... not a real change, honestly. Ceran refugees have arrived and everybody is waiting to see what the Earth has to offer to this explosive mix."

Through a cloud of static Sev could be heard sighing: "I hear ya. Then it's as bad as everybody suspects. I'm in contact with a loose collection of miners and vagrants here on the surface. Strange times. I haven't contacted my company yet, but boy-oh-boy, that will be a Pandora's box I can't wait to open and listen to all the complaints and cries for help. I'll have a proper shower with tears of brokenhearted capitalists."

"You've... quit?" Anokha asked.

Sev laughed heartily in response: "Shhhh... don't spoil the surprise. I'll try it out on my own for a while, see where it gets me. And I've never seen inhabitants of Mars so... alive. They are crawling out of their holes, and actually talking and helping each other out. At Hesperia starport they've even closed a trade deal with Cerans, a symbolic one, where they will receive platinum ingots in exchange for food grown in Mars hydroponics. But it would be the first shipment of refined ore *coming down* to Mars in a decade!"

The initial shock of hearing from someone previously thought dead was wearing out, and Iyor wasn't smiling anymore: "I am sorry if I sound discouraged, but we should be very careful. Good times always invite bad in equal amounts, and I am concerned at all the good news we are getting lately. I feel as if there's something coming our way."

Anokha and Lero gave him puzzled looks, despite their best efforts not to stare. By now he got used to those. Finally Sev cut in, as if he was present in the command room: "Listen, Iyor, it's going be alright for a while. There's nothing wrong with that. Besides, things are far from good, they are just moving in the right direction. We still have the bandits in *Holiday Inn* to keep us on our toes, before the Corporations crawl back in a couple of weeks."

"Right… about that. We were just relocating away from Deimos moon, since a probe, probably a pirate one, spotted us here. We'll see how the situation unfolds and stay on the move until Lero kicks us off the ship!" Anokha chuckled.

"Got it. I was used to sending regular reports to my employer, so I wouldn't mind continuing the habit with you guys. If you call and I don't answer… it means they've finally let me out of the purgatory to whatever lies beyond. And Iyor? Thanks for the warning, kid. I'll stay sharp, I promise you."

5.   Fireworks on the Red Planet

The working bench in the underground workshop was covered with springs, bolts and bits of alloy metal, all scattered around a moldy assembly manual for an assault rifle. It was a standard automatic model, very compact and robust, and able to operate in all environments with ease. The only real modifications to the ones they use on Earth are an integrated heat dissipation system and dampened recoil. The cartridges came with their own oxidizer, so this little thing could also operate in a vacuum although they were not very popular – a loaded gun onboard a claustrophobic spaceship makes for a light sleep.

As silly as it sounds, first guns in space were carried to fight bears. They were intended as a survival aid to be used after landings and before recovery in the Siberian wilderness, as a protection against bears and wolves.

In order to upgrade it into a sniper model, Sev inserted a longer barrel and, lacking the components for a new scope, attached his trusty monocular on the modular rail system. The smelting and assembler units he discovered in an underground cave have prepared, smelted, pressed, extruded and even 3D-printed the parts he needed to get this little base running again. He discovered that the cave was actually a half-depleted iron mine, and he was able to dig out just enough ore to get the basic process started. The good news was that the assembler module could also disassemble and decompose almost any item back to its basic building materials: reusing plastic, steel and rubber in new projects. Recycling was a way of life here on Mars, where no new investments came for over a decade, but today was the big day, with the first shipment of Ceran platinum arriving down to the Hesperia refinement center. This was a symbolic trade, but also practical, since the rare metal is used to manufacture new solar cells. Left neglected for years, all the power generators on the planet were running out of fuel. It made a lot of sense that the human interest for the red planet and the uranium isotopes in reactors have been cooling down simultaneously.

With a pleasant *click!* the magazine snapped into position, and Sev examined the rifle for any imperfections. Feeling satisfied, he left the workshop and found the communication display in the other room blinking with a new contact report. It was a shared mesh network that he could join at any time, to talk, or just eavesdrop on the chatter between scattered miners. This time it was only Gary, a miner and machinist who gave him the tip about this little base.

"Sev here, MarSafari base, over?"

"Hey, are you watching the show?"

"The show?"

"The sky is bleedin' fire, man."

"...what?!"

"There was some kind of disaster above Hesperia. The platinum shipment made it down in a million fiery pieces."

Sev blinked: "What kind of disaster? Have you heard anything from people at the refinery?"

"Yes."

Sev waited for a few moments, but no explanation was coming through. Gary was difficult to talk to, living alone and enjoying his own rhythm in life: "Well? What did they say, Gary?"

"The Accountants have returned. The Corporations, man. It's reckoning time. They came to reclaim everything. I thought I should warn you. See you man. I gotta prepare. Bye."

The line went dead, leaving him confused. The Corporations? That was downright impossible! It would take weeks to overcome the distance between Earth and Mars, not days. Gary must be losing his mind. He went back to the workshop, grabbed the rifle, took the dim-lit stairs up through the airlock and went out into the cold Martian night.

A strong wind was blowing, but otherwise the night seemed peaceful enough. He walked over to the landing pad and aimed his rifle scope at the distant glowing haze of Hesperia refinery center to the north. Shiny flakes, like final stages of fireworks, were falling over the horizon. Through his magnifying scope he could see blue lights of rocket engines on numerous small spacecraft breaking the fall, descending hastily. These were not automated ore delivery haulers. These were small, nimble craft. He didn't expect to hear any explosions in the thin atmosphere, as he watched carefully for any flashes, or signs of struggle. It was too far to be sure. The spaceships eventually landed, but the ash and burning pieces continued to drop like falling stars. Out of the blue he found the scene oddly poetic.

"What is going on out there?"

In his bones he sensed a buildup of an imminent, distant danger, and suddenly felt very alone in this tiny bunker on the ridge. He lowered the rifle and enjoyed the solitude for a while. Walking over to the rails of what used to be a tourist panorama view, he noticed for the first time a torn flag, opened up by the night gale. It was a flag of Mars, an artifact from another time. It used to be bright orange with five white interlocking circles, representing strong links with Earth. Each circle also represented a petal and together they formed a flower, a symbol of life and a vision of what Mars could become! The flag was now merely a torn rag drenched with brown dust. It was a sad thing, but on this night when the stars were falling and weapons jingling, he felt energized by what it used to represent. He took it down from the bent flagpole and put it on like a ragged poncho over his spacesuit.

He felt no less forlorn, but at least now he didn't feel out of place. Although seriously lacking social skills, Gary was a smart fox to hide. When the storm comes, embrace chaos. Anything that sticks out will be carried away. Such was the law of the red land, and anything that survived for long should be mimicked. He decided to disconnect from the meshnet, and go off the grid. Next, he should brave the wind for another night-hike to his damaged spacecraft, and get in touch with Vladivostok and ask them what is going on. His only long range communication device was the precious laser antenna fitted on the immobile MC, originally used to keep in touch with his company satellite. Perhaps the time has come to contact the Apex Corporation, and find out what was *really* going on, even if it means he has to confirm his employment status in the process.

The wind was getting stronger, breaking over the ridge and throwing up majestic formations of fine dust around him. Sev picked up a spare bottle of oxygen and set out into the loud, beautiful night.

***

The winds of Mars are fast, but due to its thin atmosphere they are not as nearly as powerful as they would be on Earth. The atmosphere got somewhat thicker with all the pollution introduced by newcomers, and yet if you leave something on the ground it would likely still be in the same spot after a decade, unmoved in the strongest gale, albeit covered with a superfine layer of cinnamon-colored dust. Nevertheless, walking in the pitch-dark surrounded by disorienting howls of wind was extremely tiring. His flashlight seemed to flicker and operate at half power with every gust of brown, smoke-like dirt thrown his way. To navigate through this mess, Sev didn't trust his senses, and instead relied on built-in suit instruments to find the way to his downed MC spacecraft.

After an hour of stumbling through the dark he finally reached it, burnt hull abruptly appearing under his unsteady light, filaments of sand seeping over its armored shell like threads of hair. Tired from a prolonged hike, he dropped behind it for protection and sighed with relief. This foul weather could obstruct a laser link, but sharing information was the only thing he could do at the moment. He crawled into the cockpit and waited as the pressurizing procedure struggled to filter out salty, toxic particles of the red planet that sneaked in.

It was never like this. His life used to be a slow routine, interrupted by stretches of simple boredom. The music and this vehicle were his only companions, and Mars used to be empty...*unimportant*. But now things were evolving so rapidly, that he had trouble making any sense of them. Here he was, in a crashed spaceship on another planet in a night storm, with no idea what was going on. All the hi-tech equipment and satellites were of no use. Actually, the communication equipment was intentionally stubbed directing you to satellites, privately owned chokepoints of information that could quite easily be turned on or off, leaving you in the dark. One would think it was all part of some evil plan, but actually it was just downsizing, compartmentalization and other long words invented to cover up a lack of real progress.

He looked at his watch and cross-referenced it with a chart attached to his control panel. The Apex satellite will not be in sight for a few more hours, and the storm would hardly allow for dynamic communication with Anokha and Iyor onboard the science vessel. He decided to wait it out in the cockpit which, damaged as it was, still contained the most important bit – his peculiar music collection. What would go well with a Mars sandstorm? He let the random chance decide his song, while he typed a single line of text as a pending message that laser antenna can push through when it manages to locate the distant science vessel.

IYOR'S PREMONITION TURNED TRUE –UNKNOWN LANDING OR RAIDING CRAFT SPOTTED OVER HESPERIA REFINERY – WHAT'S GOING ON?

6.   A message from the Frame

Click!

"Hello Iyor."

Long pause of grainy, hollow silence.

Click!

"Hello Iyor. I am not sure when this message will reach you. I'll set for the recording to be transmitted to Vladivostok. This is Edra calling, from The Frame.

Just a second..."

Click!

"Can you hear me now? I know I can count on you to still be alive at this moment, because you played this smart. But just because you were so right doesn't mean that I was wrong.

I took your advice that there could be an alternative to fighting, and we went fast from refugees, to aggressors, and then to good guys, establishing our first trade directly with Mars. The Embargo is gone, we shattered it. We felt good, unstoppable. At one point I...

Hold... hold on, my nose is bleeding..."

Click!

"Things are different now. We've come full circle, Iyor. Two hours ago, everything changed. We were waiting for the good news about the landing of our shipment to Hesperia, when we spotted a... clump approaching us, smaller than the smallest spaceship. We did nothing, just watched as it got closer to The Frame, unfolding into three figures wearing hard-shell spacesuits we've never seen before. To me they looked like babies, to be honest, all bloated and round.

Oh, if there ever was a wrong first impression...

They were soldiers, Iyor. Battle Engineers of some sort. The creeps boarded us by cutting through the hull of one of the ships in The Frame, momentarily depressurizing it and killing everyone onboard. They didn't stop there – ship by ship they went on, setting off oxygen-eating fires. We tried to fight back, madly we fell on them from all sides, but the bastards boldly constructed an automated portable machinegun, fed from our own conveyor system, to cover their back!

These bulky spacesuits they wore were unmarked, but their bones and strength betrayed them. They were planet-born, Iyor! Terrans. We are no match for them, not like this. They've coldheartedly torn us apart like toys. Passageways turned into fiery hell, with children bodies cut open, globules of blood sticking to everything. Anger got the best of me and... they shot me. Not the cool kind of wound, Iyor. It's very messy. I can't move, and the suit is getting cold and filled with... I don't know what.

Hold on a moment..."

Click!

"I'm here. The Frame is just a collection of individual small ships, docked together and moving as a single large contraption. I already gave the order for everyone to disengage, to prevent the spread of fire. Maybe we can isolate these bastards. Now, what's left of the Ceran refuge fleet is retreating to this distant orbit we prepared as a fallback point.

I am not sure if you know, but that recording you sent of your battle with Narwhal and its drones was seen by everyone here. You are the hero, Iyor. Avenger of the fall of Habakkuk. You can choose to ignore it, but it won't make a difference in people's minds. You represent something, probably the best we could offer at that moment.

You know what I want to ask you so... I need not say it. The worst thing is... I think they will get away with this sneak attack. They already got away... Can you believe that? They'll get away with everything..."

Click!

7. The Director's orders

With Sev's grim report from the surface and Edra's confession, Vladivostok turned into a nexus for bad news. But the worst one arrived in a form of a public notice transmitted throughout the Mars sector, hours after the carnage.

THIS IS A WARNING ISSUED BY CHIEF ACCOUNTING OFFICER SAND OF THE APEX CORPORATION, AS A JOINT STATEMENT FROM ITS SUBSIDARIES TO ALL THE VAGRANTS, DESERTERS AND OUTLAWS: THIS ACT OF SEDITION AND VANDALISSIM WILL NOT PASS. YOU ARE INFORMED TO LEAVE, OR YOU WILL BE APPREHENDED AND YOUR PROPERTY IMPOUNDED.

"Accountant scum! Issuing a warning *after* the bloody sneak attack! Who does he think he's fooling?" Anokha growled, as she was slipping into her spacesuit; her furious, exaggerated motions creating shuffling noises. Behind her, Iyor was donning his own ribbed spacesuit, but he was oddly quiet and difficult to read under the red light of the airlock room.

She continued: "Except the *warning* message was not really meant for us, but for people back on Earth. It was issued as a justification for the attack on The Frame and landing on the Mars refinery center, it's just that the order was wrong... nothing you can't fix when you hold the strings of mass communication. They are probably portraying themselves as defenders of the human race. Bastards!"

Iyor spoke for the first time in a while: "How did they get here so fast? They were not supposed to be here for at least a month!"

"That's what baffles me too. They must have had a fleet of ships already on route for whatever reason, but the timing is still troubling."

"Things suddenly make more sense. You remember that probe yesterday, the unidentified one that forced us to relocate?"

Anokha frowned: "You think it was them?"

"Who else? They arrived, mapped everything out and executed a simultaneous attack. I wouldn't be surprised if they boarded the *Holiday Inn* station as well."

Their heavy breathing and the buzz of the air condition unit were the only sounds in the gloomy room.They were preparing to leave *Vladivostok*, without any idea where exactly they might go in their battle-damaged bathyscaphe.

"What now?" she said, as if to herself.

Iyor took a deep breath: "You told me before that I should join *my people,* but I won't give the same advice to you. Instead I want to invite you to help me fight and crack these crazed accountants. You said it yourself that it was a good, futile fight."

Anokha leaned on his shoulder to stand up and simply said: "Let's go."

***

One hour later they finished urgent repairs to their lean, mistreated little spaceship, and then watched as the giant hull of Vladivostok slowly separated and moved away, escaping the risky Mars Theater with its thrusters glowing. Lero and the other scientists provided them with supplies and helped them as much as they could, but this was no place for an independent science vessel, so they had to return to their wandering, somewhere in the asteroid belt or beyond. Lero was searching for the origin of the alien signal. Watching that magnificent vessel with the revolving pronged section slowly depart filled them with awe. It got smaller and smaller, until its engines were just tiny dots, not bigger than any of the other stars. This left them and their ever-unfinished bathyscaphe alone in space, under Mars's watchful eye.

"Where to, Commodore Anokha?"

She looked around, as if she could somehow see very, very far with the naked eye. In reality, she saw nothing special, and yet the intangible feeling that something isn't right hasn't escaped her.

"Iyor, don't you think this director Sand is pushing a bit too hard and in all directions at the same time? It is almost as if they are trying to hide something, and serve us with a big fat bluff, hmmm? For now, let's set course for that fallback point of Ceran refugees."

8. Going native

He overslept and missed the sunrise, because there was none. The dust has thoroughly covered all the windows of his cockpit. It was the music that woke him up, a piano concerto by an unknown author. Sev massaged his face and grumbled, as the puzzling events of yesterday were revived like a bad dream.

Checking his watch, he confirmed that he will finally be in range of the Apex satellite in a few minutes, but there already was a message waiting for him, a reply to an inquiry he sent last night to his friends on Vladivostok.

WE ARE FORCED TO SEPARATE FROM VLADIVOSTOK AS THE SITUATION BECAME LESS COMPLICATED AND MORE SERIOUS. I DON'T KNOW HOW, BUT IT'S TRUE – THE JOINT CORPORATION FORCE IS ALREADY HERE, DIRECTED BY YOUR FORMER EMPLOYER, APEX.

CERAN FRAME WAS ATTACKED MOMENTS AGO! THIS COULD BE THE END OF THEIR SOJOURN. WITH VLADIVOSTOK GONE INTO HIDING, THIS FRAGILE LASER LINK BETWEEN US WILL BE SEVERED, BUT I CAN TELL YOU NOW THAT WE WON'T BE GOING ANYWHERE. IYOR AND I ARE DETERMINED TO JOIN WHOEVER OPPOSES THESE BRUTES. AND IF THERE IS NO ONE LEFT, WE WILL START OUR OWN GANG.

UNTIL WE MEET AGAIN,

ANOKHA

And that was it. All of his newfound friends – vanishing! It's as if she was trying to shield him from joining the conflict. If there are no sides, there would be no war. A simple, flawed thought, as there would be no peace either, with everyone clawing at each other all the time. One thing that she did confirm was that there was indeed a corporate fleet above Mars at this point. Something was happening.

A moment of strife bringing friction and movement, not necessarily in a good direction, but after a decade of rotting on this planet, he was willing to take a chance that this momentum can still be turned around. He sighed and did what he should have done days ago.

"Ship: attempt to establish a secure link with the Apex satellite."

"Link established. Identity confirmed–Superintendent Şevket Bulut, The Apex Corporation. Downloading sector-wide message from CAO Sand, along with an urgent appendix to your contract. Remotely *seizing control* of corporate property: one modified MC rover. Please remain in the vehicle and standby for extraction."

Horrified, Sev heard the distinct sound of a mechanical lockout throughout the cockpit!

***

Come noon, a strange shape emerged over the ridged landscape. Flat and wobbly, it floated over the northern ridge like a mirage, before diving into the flats below, raising billows of fine dust as it got closer. Two massive cylindrical thrusters suited for thin atmosphere were positioned wide apart, with a single landing claw protruding from the undercarriage. It circled around the downed MC like a cautious vulture, and then simply hovered in place for a while, as if examining the surroundings for anything suspicious. Sev recognized the craft – it was a pale yellow cargo lifter used by Hesperia refinery to pick up ore and fuel shipments from scattered mines.

A door opened on its steel belly, and a grey spacesuit-clad figure fell out with microthrusters igniting halfway down to break its fall, so it landed softly on the surface. The suit was a new one, obviously made specifically for Mars, with a hexagonal grey camouflage pattern. Sev recognized the small company logo on the stranger's sleeve, because he wore the same one on his own suit. Technically, they were colleagues.

As soon as he touched the ground, the stranger brought up a

standard compact assault rifle and advanced toward the wreckage in a trained combat stance. Sev watched his every move. His colleague approached carefully and examined the intact laser antenna module, obviously the main prize of this salvaging run. Stranger gave the thumbs up sign to his partner above, and then moved toward the front part of the wreckage. Aiming his gun at the dust covered cockpit, he hesitated for a second before pressing his wrist computer on the keypad to unlock it, quickly ducking into cover behind the gyro unit.

The cockpit was empty. Just thirty meters away, observing from a shallow ditch covered with a bleached Mars flag, Sev pulled the trigger and shot his colleague in the face, blood and glass immediately exploding in a spectacular mess, as the pressure was equalized. The muffled gunshot still buzzing in his ears, Sev dropped the sniper rifle, crawled out of his hiding spot and sprinted over to the body, which was slumped over like a doll. Working hastily, he pried out the blue hydrogen bottle from the backpack unit and clicked it into position on his own suit. He looked up. The pilot of the big steel bird started to turn the craft, closing the doors on its large belly.

Unarmed now, Sev wrestled the rifle from his colleague's death grip and jumped, fully igniting the refilled thrusters on the suit. He flew up, gunning for the diminishing opening, and made it just in time to place his arm over the sensor, blocking the door from closing completely. He was halfway inside, and continued to claw his way through the slit as the big hauler blasted off, putting tremendous force on him. With immense effort, Sev pushed through as the trapdoor closed beneath him. The hauler suddenly turned very still. Pilot has obviously abandoned the commands, realizing the intruder is already on board.

The chamber he found himself in was a small, unpressurized cargo compartment with some tiny windows on each side, and a simple, rounded door leading to the cockpit. That was it. Sev raised his rifle, checked the ammo and firing mode, and found them very familiar. It was a standard model. Then he opened the door.

There was another colleague of his in the cockpit, hiding behind the pilot seat.

"Who are you!?" she asked.

Sev didn't reply. Peeking around the doorframe, he noticed a shaky barrel of a gun extended at his direction. He crouched and sprayed the back of the pilot seat until he heard the body behind it drop down with a wet thump.

Now the only sound reaching him was the monotonous hum of the atmospheric engines. Sev stood up, and discovered that he was strangely calm, despite all the violence. His heart was beating from the running, but his mind was unexpectedly composed. He considered himself a normal, intelligent person –but when he was boxed in, he let his instincts, not his smarts, guide him through. And the most dangerous method of cornering someone was to slowly cut off their options, disarming and funneling them into an area of increased danger.

He thoroughly feared the *funnel* effect. He dreaded this creeping sense of voluntarily giving up your choices, calmly giving yourself in, until the only thing you *can* do is beg for mercy. Over time, he learned to detect the onset of this effect, and his reaction would always be to overreact and fight to get out, like an animal, before being dragged in. When his MC vehicle was remotely locked, and these goons dispatched to 'extract' him he felt that familiar crawl under his skin, and released the beastly aggression. It's over now.

It's a dog eat dog world. And in this world...

...oh, dammit!

In this dog eat dog world, he grew upto be a dog-eating *Chinaman*, the derogatory term he often used for all the loonies and aggressive madman hermits of Mars, those wild-eyed animals that the red planet has claimed for good. Now, seamlessly crossing that forbidden threshold, he has become this flag-wrapped maniac that kills when threatened, and doesn't even take time to justify it. A true, hollow survivor. He went native.

—

Fourth segment: Progress

"*Real* progress has been made."

– Chief Accounting Officer Robert Sand's opening line in his
annual report

1.   The power to change things

Things were beginning to take shape, and the perfect object to illustrate it was the irregular, wounded form of The Frame, an indestructible mobile home of the refugees from the asteroid belt. It was an ugly, temporary thing that served its purpose, made from charred-but-functional segments of a destroyed base welded together, and towed by a multitude of small ships. It was already dismantled once, to escape the destruction of The Apex sneak attack, and then cautiously reassembled here, on the fallback point, somewhere on the brink of the Mars sector.

I was standing on it courtesy of the magnetic soles of my spacesuit. Observing it from the landing platform, its construction is both hideous and glorious at the same time. Vaguely rectangular in shape, formed around the listening post module, with solar arrays and oxygen-farm tubes attached unsystematically around the hull, often blocking each other out, it resembled a floating collection of junk. And there was some junk there as well; twisted scraps of metal, damaged modules loosely attached and dragged around just because they still hold components impossible to manufacture on this exile.

And it was glorious! Each one of those tiny, submarine-shaped ships docked with The Frame contained a family of survivors, a robust speck of humanity defying the darkness around them. Born in the zero-G nurseries near the Ceres asteroid and disseminated throughout the Asteroid belt, our life was one of stark contrasts: living in crammed capsules and vast open reaches of space; suffering the scorching heat and incredibly cold shadows; listening to warm laughter and soul-bleaching silence. All this would be less painful if we didn't know better, but through colorful transmissions emanating from Earth we got a constant reminder of what it's like to live on a planet with atmosphere, magnetic field, gravity, oxygen, water and life! Our terrestrial brothers and sisters seemed ignorant of the fact that the very *sky* above them could harbor such suffering and I, on the other hand, was tortured by vivid dreams of rain, forests and seas, things I have never felt on my skin. And never will.

In a way, this conflict was just a tragic misunderstanding, as all we ever do is brutishly impose our limited experience on others.

Anokha and I, we were welcome to this floating ruin. Our reputation, like any other, was based on half-truths. They knew her as a brave smuggler who defied the trade sanctions imposed by Earth corporations, and lost her ship in the Habakkuk disaster. As a Lunar Engineering Academy graduate, her knowledge is invaluable at this moment. And out of simple necessity, they regard me as their hero. Our combat footage was now more popular than pirated action movies of Earth, because it was relevant, real, and for the first time the main actors were 'one of their own'.

The situation on The Frame was far from hopeful. We were way beyond that. Our anger was always present, but now we had a very real enemy that helped us transform it into productive hate. With our scrappy mobile base at the center, this place looked like a giant forge of war - welding fires visible on the hull of every ship. Above me a group of vindictive widows, female tribe leaders who lost all of their tribesmen, were now stripping everything away from their bathyscaphes, even rudimentary life-support, in favor of more weapons, armor and maneuverability. What worried me is that they were painting their spacefighters bright pink, fluorescent green and blinding white, as if they didn't intend to hide from conflict.

This was a strange fleet. It had no structure, no leaders and nowhere to retreat to. Our enemies don't stand a chance.

***

Anokha flew gracefully between two floating containers, before ruining her cosmic dance by clumsily landing on the ribbed hull of a docked bathyscaph. Pushing herself from one ship to another, she went deeper and deeper, until she reached the spiky Frame understructure beneath. There, she finally spotted Iyor among dozen others on the main landing platform. He noticed her and waved, face glowing with that disarming, childish smile.

As he got closer, he tapped his wrist computer to establish communication. "Anokha! I heard you set up defenses for The Frame?"

She nodded, tired but obviously satisfied: "Anything inside a thousand meter radius will be ignored, but everything beyond that will be targeted by automated turrets from a shared defense network. We have two volunteer patrols beyond the perimeter, searching for new probes sent this way. There will be no more sucker-punches. We just need to watch out for long range kinetic torpedoes. That's why I suggested regularly altering our course, despite the fuel cost."

"But aren't kinetic torpedoes banned by all conventions of war?"

She gave him a cold smile: "Conventions are set by wars, not the other way around."

"Our fuel supplies are low, you know that. Food, components, oxygen – all will be depleted soon. And even then these Apex scum won't accept our defeat. They want us out of here, so we can put pressure on our kin back in the asteroid belt. They are using us!"

Anokha pouted, looking at the big red planet above: "We can become pirates, temporarily; although I am not sure if there is such a thing as a temporary pirate. Everything here belongs to the Accountants, so anything we take will weaken them, indirectly."

"And how about we attack them – directly?" Iyor crossed his arms, waiting for her reaction.

"But we don't know anything about their location and fleet size – that's the problem."

Iyor turned away without a word and walked to the main landing platform. Confused, she followed him. The platform was used as a drop-off point, with two extendable connector rings providing a link to a set of cargo containers below. This was also the main construction area, where a team of workers was currently working on a sleek combat bathyscaphe. Iyor stepped up to one of the nearby computer terminals, then waved her over.

"When they arrived to Mars, Cerans went on to repair the communication relays and damage Narwhal left in its wake. One of the things they repaired was a little weather satellite, which is still periodically sending us footage and data. In times like this, it's the closest thing we have to a spy satellite. We know now that the *Holiday Inn Hotel* was deserted, with no sign of damage. The Pirates were probably warned ahead and abandoned it. I have no idea where they are hiding now. But take a look at what the satellite spotted in stationary orbit above the Hesperia refinery a few hours ago."

Anokha leaned in to examine the still image. With the bright surface of Mars in the background, triangular silhouettes of spaceships docked to an orbital loading platform were clearly visible. She could distinguish only a single medium-sized ship, accompanied by a neat row of smaller ones. But what really dominated the scene was the expansive scaffolding, branching out from the platform like a spider's web.

"Their fleet... it's surprisingly small. I knew they were bluffing! But what's that thing they're building? That's not a ship. It looks like a giant solar collector."

"Yes, I think so too. Any idea why they would need so much power?"

Anokha shook her head, still baffled by what she saw. Either the main fleet was elsewhere, or all this was the work of an overconfident vanguard force.

"Could be a trap," she concluded.

"Knowing that, should we attack regardless, before they have a chance to complete this massive solar array? They are getting stronger by the day, while we are getting weaker."

Anokha looked around, trying to collect her thoughts, and caught one of the nearby workers starring right at her. It was just a little girl in an oversized, charred spacesuit. One of her sleeves was hanging loose, tied in a knot, as if her arm was missing. When their eyes locked, she didn't avert her gaze. Instead, the youngster gave her a wide grin with clenched teeth, eyes gleaming with some deep-rooted impulse for life which made Anokha's skin crawl. It was more than a little scary, to feel such resolution in such a fragile package. Looking back at Iyor she had to remind herself that she was talking to a boy, a teenager, whose very existence in this conflict breached conventions about the military use of children. These space-born redefined every term thrown at them. Rules didn't apply.

"Let's put all our available forces at it." She paused, blinking as if suddenly hesitant. "Except those widows. Their drive for vengeance could turn this into a slaughter for both sides."

Iyor looked at the wild-painted ships being built next to them: "Well, you can *try* to stand in their way."

2.   Safari on Mars

The moment he flipped the antenna switch on in the MarSafari bunker, distressed messages from the mesh network started pouring in.

- *I just heard that somebody attacked an Apex patrol? A whole cargo lifter is missing. Anybody know anything?*

- *Welcome to Mars, baby! What did they expect? There are all kinds of madmen out there.*

- *Well that was stupid; they'll shoot on sight every one of us now!*

- *They can try. It's not like we are unarmed...*

Sev wondered: Did he just spark an uprising, or was something like this bound to happen sooner or later? But this was not his war and he had no plans to be involved in this *thing* he happened to start. Still, it was a pleasant surprise to hear the once-compliant and scattered locals of the red planet band together in the face of a common threat. *Me against my brother. Me and my brother against the neighbors. All of us against the foreigner!*

Being treated as a foreign entity and not the rightful owner will probably come as a shock for the Corporations. Being estranged for so long, they started to believe their contracts still held some power over this unprofitable planet and its band of stranded survivors. You can always count on times of strife to bring about progress and shatter illusions set by decades of peaceful stagnation. Tomorrow morning, the Apex mercenaries will look out to a calm Mars vista and they will have doubts about their mission here.

To avoid the inevitable dragnet, he needed to stay mobile. Looking at what was left of his MC rover/spaceship, he wondered if the wreckage is even remotely useful, or was he simply being overly sentimental to drag it all the way here for repairs. The thing belongs in a museum, if there was such a thing on Mars. It would definitely make a fine addition to the MarSafari venue. But all the tourists are gone, and instead there was a private army that will be looking for it.

Right now, he had more assets than he could control: a broken MC, a big cargo hauler with a bloodied cockpit and an entire bunker-base. The smart thing would be to get rid of everything and hide in the bunker, but sooner or later someone like Gary is going to talk about it and, with its illegal assembler unit, it could be marked for search. If only he had a team of people he could trust now. Anokha and Iyor came close, but they did their best to push him out of this conflict, as if that was possible. When real people are not available, engineers turn to drones. And he knew where to find one.

With a sad look on his face, he picked up a set of tools and set out to the base of the ridge, where the little green rollbot was still stuck in his eternal ascent.

"Sorry, little guy. You're getting a bigger body, that's all."

Green sparks flew as he dismantled the thing, neatly sorting the components on the rocky ground. He picked up a remote-control module, the programmable heart of this drone which contained rudimentary artificial intelligence, and then made his way back to the landing platform where a stolen cargo lifter aircraft was waiting. He carefully inserted the drone module into the main controller slot under the cockpit. There was no apparent change, but he could now remotely direct the lifter, or set a waypoint for its autopilot. Not really a solid replacement for a trained pilot, but it will do.

Biting his lip, he walked over to what was left of his original Mars vehicle – the MC rover, and soothingly placed his hand on the cracked chassis: "You look terrible, old friend."

What a solid machine! He set out to cut off every twisted piece of metal, only to uncover more misshapen understructure beneath.

The damage ran deep. Grunting, Sev continued to peel off ruined segments, until he was left with barely a half of the original vehicle. Now the *real* work begins. Working feverishly for the next two hours, his hands shaking from exhaustion, he was finally able to witness MC's third functional reincarnation into a single-cockpit, four-wheeled light rover. He used the assembler unit downstairs to manufacture the missing components, but he kept the oxygen generator and the precious laser antenna from its original setup.

As the sun set down, he realized the time for repairs was over, and not just because of the dying light. Over a distant ridge to the east he spotted a set of searchlights on a low flying vessel, meticulously scanning the area. Without a moment's hesitation he jumped into the MC, and remotely ordered the cargo hauler to pick them up. A hasty change of plans, but he didn't want to be here when the Apex search teams arrive, looking for the missing vehicle. The newly-made drone flawlessly executed his command; Sev watched it rise and hover above them, slowly lowering its magnetic gear to gently press and lock on top of the MC.

"Here goes!" He set the autopilot coordinates approximately fifty kilometers to the west, far away from those searchlights.

Momentarily the thrusters roared, the suspension squeaked, and then they were in the air, carried by the obedient drone hauler. He held to his seat as they dove into the thick darkness of the valley below. One more night spent under the stars, in some repaired vehicle on a planet that doesn't want him there. Sev realized he is instinctively gripping the wheel, even though he handed the controls over to the flying drone. The Late Space Age is coming to an end; there was movement all around him, and he just wanted to stay alive long enough to see what comes afterwards.

3. Raja

Frame>"Opening up battle coordination channel from the Frame control room. This is Anokha. All squadrons – report!"

Composite 1> "Heavy squadron reporting , Keira here."

Composite 2> "Iyor with squadron 2. We are right behind you."

Composite 3> "This is Gemma with the widow squadron. We are ready for action and may I add... thank you for letting us join this ride."

Frame> "Don't let us down. We need you to work together with us, without any wild attacks."

Composite 3> "Oh, I have a good reason to get through this alive. I'm pregnant."

Frame> "Well... I think what you just said sums up the current situation for Cerans. Good luck everyone. They know we are coming, but we outnumber them in this attack."

Like blue fireflies, hundreds of small ion thrusters ignited simultaneously around The Frame. Bathyscaphes, armed barges, streamlined fighters of all sizes, and zebra-painted spaceships with exposed cockpits started to separate into three loose groups. As one, this ragtag flotilla turned toward Mars and blasted off, rotating and spinning as if showing off, or simply learning the controls of their newly modified spacecrafts.

Frame> "Composite 1, pick up speed and breach through. Take out their small combat craft and avoid the medium-sized frigate. Iyor with his squadron will be right behind you, as the second wave. Widows will fall in last, to make sure this is not a trap. Try to avoid damage to the loading station and the solar collector, so just focus on their defenses."

The heavily armored spearhead consisted of thirty-two flat, sluggish barges bristling with missile and machinegun turrets. With their long barrels sticking out from the stern, they resembled a band of metal hedgehogs. They were followed by a large force of light bathyscaphes, equipped with nimble hydrogen thrusters, and finally a small force of stripped down, heavily-armed fighters of the third squadron.

Composite 2> "We will limit the thrust to 60% in order to form attack waves."

Composite 1> "Got it. We'll push through without turning for a second run. Hopefully we'll lure some of them, and that's when we need you."

Composite 2> "Count on it!"

As they picked up different speeds to cross thousands of kilometers in their parabolic trajectory, squadrons got separated by immense distances. Mars was getting bigger with each passing second, its deadly junk belt clearly visible now. At first there was chatter on short distance communication, as tribes formed tight groups inside each squadron, but soon it was replaced by a tension-pumped silence. There was no cheering and no gloating on this doomed flotilla. Having lost his whole tribe, Iyor's place oughta be in the back with the widows, but instead he tried to serve as an exposed anchor for the second assault wave.

***

Composite 1> "We are approaching the outer reaches of the Clutter. If we run into dense debris we will have to turn on automated turrets to clear the path, even if this exposes our approach. Stay alert."

Flat shapes of the first wave slipped through the shimmering clouds of dust and particles without raising any alarms. Armed barges formed a tight formation in preparation for the battle ahead.

Composite 1> "Contact! We are entering their defense network. We have satellites, probes and drone mines."

Frame> "Avoid if possible, and press on to the loading platform. Faster ships of our flotilla won't have a problem with the mines, so engage them only if they get in your way."

Composite 1> "There is a lot of activity here! I am picking up a multitude of unidentified signals in the Clutter belt, probably from all the floating debris that's still powered-up. I don't like this."

Composite 2> "We are right behind you, Keira. Stay focused."

Numerous spacecraft of Iyor's second wave were entering the outskirts of Clutter like a cloud of bees, their hydrogen thrusters already ignited for quick maneuvering. Once inside, it was as if they entered a dark forest teeming with strange wildlife, dozens of radio signals and spinning wreckages buzzing all around them like crickets and frogs. This was a good place to set an ambush. Ignoring the radar contacts, he tried to visually locate any active thrusters, but this was just a junkyard. He kept examining larger segments and found the shape of some of them odd, but they just seemed to drift harmlessly, forgotten for decades.

Composite 1> "Loading platform in sight. Apex fighters and frigate are on the move."

Frame> "Initiate rapid deceleration maneuver. Iyor, be there to provide cover for the barges."

Composite 2> "We're on it."

Frame> "Widows, is everything clear in the back?"

Composite 3> "Everything's calm, but we are still far from Clutter."

First explosion came when one of the drone mines propelled itself into a collision course with the barges. It was silently cleaved in half by machinegun fire, but then it spewed out a multitude of tiny warheads that detonated after a few seconds, creating a wall of deadly fireworks that sent ripples through the debris. The barges opened their tight formation to avoid the spectacle and to line up for an attack run.

The loading station ahead was a large, disc-shaped object with a row of containers stacked under it, and spider-like cranes dominating its top side. Two broad hauler-ships with powerful thrusters used to lift goods from the surface of Mars were docked with it. Extending from the main platform, a huge segmented solar collector was under construction – its purpose unknown. And behind it all, a knife-shaped frigate bearing the Apex Corporation white stripes was slowly rising, accompanied by a squadron of fighters.

Composite 1> "Engaging enemy fighters. From the looks of it, their flagship is a fabricator frigate. It's only lightly armed."

Frame> "Don't be fooled, it's still a big ship. Steer clear of it, and take out its escort."

Composite 1> "With pleasure!"

Assault barges advanced in a line, laying a hail of fire at incoming Apex fighters. Hits were expectedly rare at this distance, but after they released a salvo of rockets the battle quickly degraded into a confusing firefight between automated turrets tracking extraordinary fast targets. Sparks, explosions and broken chunks of armor mixed with the floating junk. There was no more order, all formations were lost, but barges managed to push through without any collisions. After the initial clash, there was no clear victor. Apex fighters proved surprisingly durable, many of them perforated but still functional.

Composite 1> "They have new modules!"

Frame > "What... what new modules?"

Composite 1> "Hrrrnngh... They have different cockpit modules!

Bigger. Better armored. They are using the same modular construction, only they've upgraded! We are hitting them, but they're not going down."

Composite 2> "The second wave will arrive in a moment. Hold tight!"

Out of the void, at first indistinguishable from all the debris, came the bulk of Ceran refuge fleet: disorganized, lethal and lean. Each cluster of bathyscaphes was a tight tribe which executed complicated maneuvers sharing the same heartbeat. They moved counter-intuitively, avoiding the fire while unconsciously exposing the enemy – working not as a team, but rather as an elemental force. Battle soon turned brutal, with burning hydrogen leaks and pilots in torn spacesuits thrown out of their demolished spacecraft. Apex frigate steered into a defensive position over the solar collector as if to shield it, releasing a salvo after salvo of fast, unguided rockets at an isolated cluster of ships. Stray projectiles already pierced its hull, setting off small geysers of leaking oxygen and fire.

Composite 2> "Anokha, I have this bastard CAO Sand trying to contact us. Should I push his communication through?"

Frame> "He wants to distract us. We will contact them when they are disarmed."

The momentum pushed both assault waves through, so now the two fleets were temporary separated and aligning for a second run. Apex defenses were in shambles. Drone mines were depleted, most gun emplacements destroyed, and the frigate damaged. Corporate fighter squadrons – although upgraded – were eventually outmaneuvered by agile Ceran spacecraft. Now most of them were disabled and being tugged closer to the platform for quick repairs, while the remaining forces braced for the final charge.

Composite 3> "Widows are here. We are entering the Clutter belt for the joint attack."

Frame> "We have them pinned. Disable their combat craft and we can end this."

Composite 3> "Hold on. There is a capital ship bulldozing its way through the debris, heading for the platform. We don't need radar – we can actually see it! It's a cruiser."

Frame> "A cruiser?! That's well above our firepower. Okay, we'll figure out later how it got here. Squadrons 1 and 2, finish the attack on the platform defenses and pull out to the fallback point. Widows, try to distract the cruiser without engaging it directly!"

Composite 3> "Aye, aye. We'll buy you some time."

Assault barges completed the fuel-costly turn and were now advancing below the platform, seeking partial cover. Mingling between them were clusters of smaller bathyscaphes positioning themselves for the final assault. Even though the initial clash lasted only a couple of minutes, the strain placed on the pilots during the complicated maneuvers was immense.

They blasted under the platform, taking potshots at the frigate's belly from underneath their solar collector. One of the rockets made it through and the explosion disconnected the main thruster segment, immobilizing the big ship. In the mayhem of battle, barges made brief stops to snatch cargo containers, while bathyscaphes spread out to collect disabled craft and rescue stranded pilots. Like the wind they swept through every crevice, wreaking massive destruction before retreating.

Now they could see a menacing shadow of a single battlecruiser coming their way, bits of debris bouncing off its reinforced prow as it confidently advanced. Its sleek, elongated hull with no openings or windows and slanted, matte-grey armor marked it as a combat vessel of immense firepower.

Composite 3> "It's not responding to our provocations, and now it's launching a fighter squadron. Get out of its way, now! We will cover your retreat."

Composite 2> "We are towing our wounded pilots and disabled craft. Our speed will be reduced."

Exhausted, the pilots altered course to evade the danger, while the colorful bathyscaphes of the Widow squadron feigned elaborate attack runs on the approaching behemoth. The cruiser seemed to ignore the bait and tilted to the side in order to fully use its main thruster. A short burst of what seemed like a huge, controlled explosion behind it illuminated the junk field like a small star.

Composite 1> "It's chasing us!"

Frame> "We have no choice. All squadrons – disperse throughout the junk belt, and then regroup at the fallback point. Our sluggish barges from Squadron 1 will have a hard time getting out of there. Escort them to safety and use only short distance communication to avoid detection. I am closing the battle channel now. Anokha out."

***

Attack on the Apex platform proved difficult and, with our flotilla spread thin through a deadly field of debris, coupled with being chased by a battlecruiser, it was too early to call it a success.

"This is squad leader Iyor. It cannot pursue all of us, but once we separate, you'll be on your own! Form teams: one tribe per barge. Stay close and protect it from pursuing fighters. See you at the fallback point."

On the display wall around me I observed as teams of light bathyscaphes separated from our main group like splinters and huddled around each of the assault barges. Like a flower our formation opened up, and then vanished, blending in with the spinning scrap. I was alone in the cockpit. It felt strange and too silent in here without Anokha as my copilot in the backseat. One of the barges towing a blue cargo container was traveling without an escort, so I steered closer to it and was immediately joined by three more ships. Matching its speed, I allowed the barge to lead the way. The cruiser pressed on, scattering our flotilla before it. I could see a single enemy fighter-squadron, led by a larger red-and-black spaceship with white stripes, locked in a vicious battle with the Widows.

Those that hesitate and turn back to help them will run into the cruiser's range. Widows better retreat fast; they've bought us enough time. As we moved deeper into the Clutter belt to evade the chase, I realized we were in an unknown, dangerous territory, and without communication we wouldn't be able to call for help.

It's going to be a perilous journey back to The Frame.

Our little splinter group has switched off all antenna signals. We were flying slow and dodging debris, trying to stay as close to each other as possible, otherwise we might get lost in this graveyard. The cruiser was slowly gliding through above us, as if searching for movement. Unnoticed, we moved away through the gloom.

I turned my bathyscaphe into a spin, giving a visual signal for the group to accelerate. The sooner we got out of here, the better. Twisted shapes floated around us: pipes, glass, and even a clump of refined ore ingots from some shipment that never made it through. Occasionally we saw a glint of something whizzing by, each one of those lethally fast moving pieces of junk an instant death to the unlucky. Machinegun turrets on our barge nervously acquired and locked on to passing targets, but so far they remained quiet since nothing was heading our way.

We have left the Apex platform and the cruiser behind us. I wondered if others had such a smooth escape through this treacherous area. This place was no good. Fragments of spaceships, cargo and...

A faint light of an ion thruster among the junk, but now it's gone.

Have we stumbled upon one of our own? My gut told me this was something else. An irregular, asymmetric segment seemed to be slowly spinning, as if to face us. I distanced myself from the barge, igniting the tactical thrusters. My teammates immediately followed, but they were not the only ones to respond to my signal. Rockets flared past us from above as the machineguns on the barge opened fire, exploding some of them before they reached their target.

I could see them now. Horsemen pirate ramships, disguised as junk, with deeply-set, concealed thrusters. My teammates springed into action, fanning out as I tried to count their numbers. It was hard. Horseman pirates are clever, crazed survivors of the bleak, deep space beyond the asteroid belt. The distance has made them detached and brutally practical. 'Civilized' inner sectors of Mars and Earth was not ready for their return.

I spotted two, three... four segments of junk, all moving closer with their characteristic, axe-like prow used for primitive – but effective – ramming. The Clutter will limit our maneuverability here. More rockets exploded, sending shockwaves through my bones. My rocket turret has already acquired a target, so I allowed it to shoot at will, while I steered clear of fire from our barge. Tracer projectiles were flashing everywhere, raining hard on armor plates around my enclosed cockpit. The jagged ramships were gunning for the barge, but all their weapons were aimed at its escort, spewing heavy flak. It was as if they didn't want to damage the plunder.

Being close enough for short-range communication I screamed into the headset: "Drop the cargo! It's not worth it. That's all they want."

But one of the ramships already blasted past me and clipped the barge, narrowly missing its critical section. They both spun out of control after the impact, and I could see the large cargo crate was detached and drifting away.

"Forget the cargo! Form on the barge and let's move out of here."

As if that was all they wanted, the ramships whizzed around to provide cover, one of them closing in on the loot. Luckily, our barge was still in one piece and we huddled close to it, leaving this dreadful place behind.

***

An hour later, at the fallback point on the outskirts of the junk belt, we connected with the remnants of our weary flotilla. Some of them have already left toward The Frame, towing those that need urgent medical help. Barges and bathyscaphes carried disabled craft, nothing that couldn't be fixed, but some of us haven't made it through yet. Finally I saw them coming, last group led by the colorful widow spaceships.

Their leader, Gemma, hailed me: "Iyor, we couldn't get everyone out."

"Were you attacked by pirates?"

"What? No, it was that damn ace pilot."

"The one from the cruiser perhaps? The red-and-black heavy fighter?"

Gemma hissed: "That one. Curse his black soul. We simply couldn't keep up. All of us were on it, but he dodged away to mow down and cripple retreating targets. Then he came back at those moving in to rescue them. Demon!"

My hands were shaking from fatigue. The attack –followed by this unexpectedly long, grueling return home – bested our machines and our will, yet despite all our efforts some of us were still left behind. We disabled the frigate and destroyed most of the Apex fleet, but we were far from being even after that sneak attack by their sappers. And now this advanced cruiser appeared out of nowhere! Their ability to move ships around was pure magic.

4.   Trampled flower

The cockpit of the little rover was packed with supplies, tools and weapons. Sev was sitting in the center of this mess, like a king on a crooked throne. Two rifles, ammo canisters, hand drill, stacks of iron ingots, aluminum food packages, water bottles, oxygen bottles, hydrogen bottles and a torn, bleached flag hanging over the doorway leading to a tiny sleeping chamber. The rover was currently traversing a thirsty patch of ashen land known as Hesperia Planum. He has hidden the carrier drone in a low crater, fearful that it could be easily spotted during the daytime. It was still remotely controlled, so hopefully he can bounce the laser antenna signal off one of the abandoned satellites and call on it if he needs to quickly relocate.

So far, his little MC rover was perfect. Not much was left of the original, beastly design created to wrestle with Mars landscape with ease. But machines evolve too: Sev was getting smarter, and more in tune with this planet. He constructed this tiny rover not to fight the terrain, but merely glide over it. It was low, wide and featured a smaller set of wheels. Overall it resembled a short, flat centipede. The settings of the suspension module were fully editable, so they could handle the surface and gravity of Mars, Moon and Earth with simple adjustment. At the moment all he wanted was to stay out of sight until he could grasp what's going on, and this vehicle was perfect for the task.

To stay alive, he had to stay on the move. But to get any sort of info, he needed to get in touch with the locals, or his friends in the sky. People always flock to the high ground. It's in their genes. A place that's overlooking the plains is where he would find others. Encounters were always a gamble on the red planet, but recent events sent ripples that spawned some kind of unity. In a way, this strife was good for Mars. To his right he could see the only mountain around. Actually, it was an eroded, low-lying volcano called Tyrrhenus Mons, but it was known as Dandelion, because of the numerous flat-floored valleys radiating from the central depression, which could be seen from orbit. He steered the rover in that direction.

The day was clear and perfect, without a breath of wind. He used his monocular to examine every suspicious speck in the sky. As he expected, there was a lot of activity in the direction of the Hesperia Refinery. Flat hauler ships were going up, towing cargo containers, while the empty ones were descending. Tiny dots of thrusters could be seen even from this distance. In front of him, the Dandelion Volcano looked like a rusty wall, a kilometer tall and forty kilometers wide, curving slowly on both sides. He searched for any kind of habitat and spotted a crane-like structure in the valley ahead, but it was too far to make out any details. Out of caution, he altered his course to barely avoid the landmark.

"What the hell?" he muttered upon noticing other cranes and poles, sticking like ribs from ash, scattered in a wide area.

His suspicion was replaced by explorer's curiosity. These were some kind of ruins, but why wasn't this place picked clean already? Now he passed by a long twisted girder, erected and supported by other metal scrap. Someone had intentionally raised this thing as a flagpole, but there was no banner. Instead, there was simply a white ideogram painted on top. People here used distorted Chinese ideograms or Japanese kanji as a sort of code, this recently invented Mars lingo with words nobody really knew how to pronounce. But the message was clear. It stood for: 'Bad Place'.

Sev frowned and looked around. There was not much here. No central hub and no obvious danger.

"Oh."

The Dandelion crater. Fresh wreckage.

"Oh."

This must be what's left of the Narwhal after it broke apart and plummeted to Mars. This was his handiwork. He was surprised to see anything sticking out from the surface. The atmosphere was thin and wouldn't burn everything, but the impact must have been tremendous, flattening the structure down to a pulp. There was nothing here, except evil spirits of half dead robotic pilgrims that followed the cursed ship to its doom.

And still, he was curious to find some kind of closure. His little rover made its way over the scarred ground, passing unrecognizable molten modules. Bits and pieces impacted over a wide area, creating small craters and plowed lines with scattered rocks. The rover fitted snuggly into one such canal as he brought it to a stop. Sev picked up a sniper rifle and tied that ragged flag as a cloak, preparing for a little stroll outside.

This was a bad place alright. Nothing moved, but twisted arms of automated turrets, bent antennas and armor sheets like scales from a big metal dragon were scattered all around, sticking out like teeth from the flat, disturbed ground. There was a sort of high ground where a larger piece hit, so he kicked some sand over MC to camouflage it better, then continued his way on foot. He walked slowly, absorbing the destruction.

Something moved in his peripheral vision, so he quickly kneeled, whipping his cloak around. It was a ship, appearing so suddenly as if it was dropping directly from the sky above. Sev ducked under a perforated plate of armor and waited. It was coming down fast, finally blasting pillars of flame from two large thrusters. He could see now that it boasted the Apex white stripes design on a distinctive red-and-black color scheme. It was a large spacefighter, heavily armed and with plenty of thruster power. It made a half-circle descending maneuver, and a cloud of raised dust obscured its point of landing.

The newcomer has touched down on the same spot he was headed to. People always flock for that little bit of high ground controlling the plains. Without thinking too much, Sev ran closer, using billows of dust as cover. Upon reaching the slope of the crater he dropped on all fours and crawled to the top, waiting for the cloud to disperse.

Slowly, the intimidating shape of the modern spaceship emerged. The cockpit module was something new, double the size of a regular one, with reinforced triangular windows and aerodynamic lines. Different-sized barrels protruded under each wing, while a row of thruster nozzles dotted the sides of its armored hull. The color pattern was bold, as if to intentionally attract attention, which isn't something you want to do in combat, unless you know what you're doing. From the look of it, it has seen battle recently, but the damage was superficial.

The doors on its bullet hole ridden belly opened, and out rolled a strange duo of man and machine. The pilot was wearing a specialized suit, with a bulbous helmet packed with visual search instruments. He was unarmed, but he was followed by a simple three-wheeled drone that scanned the surroundings with its machinegun turret.

Sev ducked. It's difficult to hide from drones. They see in every direction at the same time. But still, he was curious. *What are they doing here?*

Carefully, Sev peeked over. The pilot was kneeling. He picked up a handful of sand and let it sift through his fingers.

What's he doing over there?

But his curiosity was gradually being replaced by something else. Sev *wanted* that ship. It was not greed or bloodlust; he simply had newfound meaning for what constitutes right of ownership. Outside of his fighter, this pilot was nothing. The Corporations branded their logo and stripes on stuff to mark their turf, but out here it was as meaningless as their contracts, signed and verified on another planet. You can own only what you really need. And Sev needed that space-ready ship –not to fight a one-man-war, but simply to stay alive for a little longer, so he could see the dawn of the new age. He had a tingling sensation that it was very close. Maybe he *was* going utterly mad.

The guardian drone presented an obstacle, though. It was a small, twelve segment unit with exposed internal structure. A well placed shot to the power grid would disable it, but a miss would summon an overwhelming reaction from the persistent machine. He carefully aligned his sniper rifle, and just as he was about to take aim – he was spotted! Machinegun turret rotated in an instant, but stopped half way through, as its power core was shattered with Sev's instinctive snapshot.

"Hold it!" Sev yelled as he stood up, taking aim at the startled pilot.

The pilot looked back at his crippled robot, then straight at Sev. He stood up, defiantly dispersing what was left of the ashen dust in his hand.

Advancing carefully, with the smoking gun aimed straight at the pilot's throat, he wondered if there were more corporate goons inside the ship.

His target spoke first, with the voice deep and distorted by atmospheric modulators: "I was warned this planet was crawling with brigands. Where did you steal that Apex suit?"

"The suit... is mine."

"Ah... so you are one of those disgruntled traitors setting traps for our people?"

Sev tilted his head with a mocking smile: "What *people?* You are just a corporate hireling who doesn't belong he–"

Then he spotted something very strange. In front of the pilot there was a small pile of sand, and nested on top it was a glass tube with a real flower in it. A flower!

Backing off a little bit, Sev exclaimed: "Whoa! What's going on here?"

The mysterious pilot just stood there, attentive. Then he lifted a gold-mirrored layer of his visor, and an unfamiliar Indian face with dreadlocks and wires intermingling around it appeared: "I came here to avenge my sister, and you are just a distraction that cannot stop me."

"Sister?" A piece of the puzzle fell into place. "Then you are... from the Jágr family?"

The pilot gave him a confused look: "I am Raja Jágr, yes. How did you conclude that?"

"Your sister is Anokha, right?" Sev watched as Raja nodded, dumbfounded. "She survived the crash of the Narwhal. She wasn't on it!"

Raja blinked, his limp lips half-opened.

Sev lowered his rifle: "Your sister is probably alive, if Apex didn't get her yet."

"You are lying."

"Am I?"

Raja turned his head a little, still starring back with a mix of fear and bewilderment, as if listening to a convincing heretic: "Where is she now?"

"Nothing comes free. How come the Apex fleet was so conveniently close to Mars?"

"Close? I was on Earth just two days ago."

Now it was Sev's turn to act puzzled: "How is that?"

"Nothing comes free. I won't back down until I find Anokha.

When I heard about the Ceran attack on Mars and saw the pictures of the crash site, I gladly accepted the contract to get here. Where is she?"

"Is that what you were told? Anokha is with the Ceran refugees right now, and not as a prisoner. It wasn't them that brought chaos to Mars, it was this accursed ship!" He pointed at the broken pieces littered about.

Raja covered his face with a gloved hand: "It would be easier for everyone if you are just lying. Who are you?"

"I'm the one holding the gun. Now answer me: how did Apex get here so fast?"

Raja lifted his chin up: "Go and ask Director Sand at Hesperia refinery yourself. I am not a traitor like you."

"Not even if it means saving your sister?"

"You don't hold her. I will deal with the Cerans on my own."

"Then you are of no use to me." Sev lifted the long barrel of his sniper rifle and aimed at that defiant smirk of his. "See, Raja, you are everything wrong with this world. You sign the contract, believe the lies, keep your stupid honor and kill when ordered to without a moment of doubt. That comes later, but then you are powerless to change the past. You are a silent, stupid, vengeful, deadly majority that's easily manipulated by those smarter than you. I hate every last one of you devoted robots!"

Raja stood there without a word, jaw muscles coiling from tension.

Sev slowly lowered the weapon, exhaling like a bull with nostrils opened wide. He was still just standing there and breathing heavily when Raja turned away, dragged the damaged drone through the colorless sand back into the spaceship and closed the door without looking back. Moments later, two massive thrusters rotated for liftoff, blasting small rocks and dust at Sev, his flag-cape flapping violently. With a terrible noise, the steel machine left towards the stars riding a wave of fire, leaving him alone among the twisted junk.

At his feet was a tilted jar, a single white flower enclosed within. It looked so fragile.

"Director Sand, Hesperia Refinery then." he said in a guttural voice. "I could fight these replaceable morons all day, or simply take out the chief accountant. The contract-pusher. The devil of Mars."

5. Reunion in wartime

When I exhaled, the bubbles went up, racing through the water until they reached the surface and vanished. It was cold. I pushed myself up, and then I remembered I don't know how to swim. The silvery surface seemed to be slipping away. There was an onset of panic as I begun to suffocate. I woke up.

These were my dreams of Earth, like transmissions picked up from afar while I slept. Dreaming in open space is dangerous. As the Bedouin say: 'When you sleep in a house, your thoughts are as high as the ceiling, but when you sleep outside they are as high as the stars.' And still, it could all fit in our eye, in our mind. We could do this; we could survive out here. We were not built for this, but we are adapting. The process was already underway, so why can't they just leave us in peace? I decided that the moment we stopped having these Earth dreams would be the moment we could finally move on.

I donned my suit, and just as I clicked the helmet into place there was a silent alarm signal, a blinking blue light that brought a surreal light show to my tiny cabin onboard The Frame. This was not a major alert, but merely a sign for me to get to the control room. As I silently glided through the central arching hallway of our mobile base, I could see people sleeping in small hammocks in other rooms. The place smelled of sweat, blood and disinfectant. We were tired, but hopeful at least.

And here was my addition to The Frame that raised many a brow. A real window! Something of a debauchery, and yet a favorite gathering place on our station. It was a mirrored sheet of reinforced glass, about a meter wide, offering a view of the glorious structure of our mobile base. Through it, I could observe workers over at the construction platform as they analyzed new modules that we towed in from the attack on the Apex loading platform. They were made from same basic components, so our assembler units could break them apart, copy the exact design and multiply it. And with the refined ore our barges snatched, we could now upgrade our refugee fleet.

Passing multiple doors that marked detachable segments, I found my way through one of the crammed tunnels to the central hub.

***

Under a dome of illuminated buttons and displays, Anokha was sitting alone, slouched over a computer terminal, while her fingers were dancing feverishly over the keyboard as a long line of code grew across the screen.

"Hey, Commodore." Iyor appeared next to her, smiling.

"Iyor! What time is it?"

"It's time you finally get some sleep. You've been here for three shifts."

With a furrowed brow she muttered something incomprehensible as a reply. The sound of buttons clicking went on, but then another sound interrupted it: enemy alert!

With her hand hovering over the overall alert button, Anokha immediately snapped to attention: "We have a hostile inbound. Carrying Apex ID tag. Arming first line of defense rockets."

"They've found us!"

"It's a single ship. Probably a scout. I am converging our patrols to cut off its escape."

"It's not going away – it's heading straight at us. But it's too slow for a kinetic torpedo." Iyor shook his head. "Should I assemble a squadron to intercept it?

"It got into automated defense range. A missile is already intercepting it."

They watched as the impact countdown timer quickly went down to zero and then started to raise again, a sign of a clear miss. The radar blimp swayed only a little bit before continuing down its trajectory, constantly decelerating.

"Dodged it!" Iyor exclaimed. "Can you bring the visual?"

Main display shone with the distinctive red-and-black pattern of a large fighter, tilted to one side as it brought its thrusters for a deceleration maneuver.

"It's slowing down, not accelerating for an attack run." Anokha said, puzzled.

Iyor frowned: "No, it must be a trap. That Ace pilot killed and maimed a good portion of our flotilla over Mars. All the Widows couldn't contain him. I'm telling you, it's a trap."

The enemy fighter slowed down to a near stop, now a perfect target for automated defense and Anokha nodded: "I have it locked with my turrets. Scramble a squadron and, if it doesn't pose a threat, escort it to the construction platform. I'll meet you there."

"On it!" He said, and stormed out of the control chamber.

***

Dark barrels and missile-tube heads tracked the intruder on its approach to the landing pad, blinking with green docking lights. The menacing ship unfolded its landing gear and touched down. Two armed bathyscaphes moved in to hover above it. The ramp on its belly was lowered, and a solitary figure walked out to the center of the platform, under the watchful eyes of a dozen armed workers, ducking behind cover. Their blades and compact rifles were gleaming red under Mars's light.

Holding his knife at the ready, Iyor approached the unarmed stranger, closely followed by Anokha. As they got closer, the newcomer lifted his mirrored visor to present a stern, resolute face.

Just as Iyor opened his mouth to speak, Anokha graciously walked past him to hug her brother.

They stood there, locked in a firm embrace, and Raja allowed himself a serene smile. Anokha wasn't smiling; she looked limp, like a sleeping child ready to be taken to bed. Odd moments passed, during which Raja and Iyor exchanged glances, as if silently assuring each other that there is no harm. The others around him were still unconvinced, many of them still nursing wounds from their recent battle.

Finally, Raja gently lifted his sister and separated from her arms: "Listen, we don't have much time. I've come to ensure your safe passage out of here. They know you are here, and the cruiser *Zamora* is already approaching for a surprise attack. But nobody has to die. Please, just leave." His voice faltered by the end in an honest plea.

Iyor looked at the gathering Cerans around him, but Anokha spoke first, with a sad smile on her face: "Leave where, Raja? Back to a corporate oligarchy and autistic Earth? Or leave for the asteroid belt, where we will slowly turn into outlaws and pirates just to stay alive?"

Iyor just watched. In essence, she presented their options well, and both of them were just prolonging the inevitable decline.

"Then I surrender to you." Raja said, with a formal bow. "I realized that I came here to exact vengeance, and in doing so I only gave reason for reprisal. This wheel will never stop turning. But you are alive, Anokha. While this makes me happy, it also marks me as a very stupid, blind person."

He sighed and bowed his head. Somehow, he shrank in size.

Iyor nodded: "Thank you for the warning. We will be ready for this attack. Apex is pushing too hard, and in every direction. But because of this they will fall into every ambush, and spring every trap we set for them." He deactivated the magnetic soles of his suit and jumped, flying away to his bathyscaphe.

"How did you know I was with the Cerans?"

"A scruffy hermit I've met on the surface of Mars told me." Raja shook his head, as if recollecting a bizarre memory. "And I believed him!"

6.   Hesperia

There were streets here on Mars! Real streets, with real buildings and real colonists inside. Flying low over decrepit suburbs of what used to be the first colony, Sev traced a pale line between the ruins that was leading straight to the spaceport. The area ahead was teeming with activity. A fleet of cargo haulers, much like the one he was currently piloting, were pouring in and congregating over the refinery complex. They were towing bits of cargo and junk, carelessly dropping them in the central collector, a funnel-like tower surrounded by smoking spires.

Apex Sappers. Recruited and trained on Earth for the sole purpose of recycling the entire planet. The Hesperia Refinery used to be operated by local employees, collecting ore from scattered independent miners and shipping the product with drone lifters to the loading platform in orbit. The scope of work has increased since Apex arrived. Squatters were evicted, and a controlled perimeter was established around the spaceport with a line of automated turrets and patrolling drones.

In a stolen hauler, and with his shabby MC rover in tow, he blended in perfectly with all the other vultures. It will hopefully be enough to get him inside the controlled area. He was approaching the cloudy refinery complex, when another hauler passed over him, carrying a six-wheeled miner rover riddled with bullet holes. The cockpit was cracked open, and a dead driver was dangling out, still strapped to his seat. Down the funnel it went, along with the rest.

Sev was so stunned by the sight that he didn't notice they were already flying over the controlled zone. Breaching through a cloud of smoke above the main collector, he discovered a huge, frigate-sized spaceship moored on the main landing pad behind it. It seemed to have sustained battle damage, layers of its octagonal-shaped armor scales chipped away. A curtain of scaffolding walled it off as dozens of vehicles flocked in like ants, carrying freshly manufactured components from the refinery complex. He recognized the design of the frigate. It was a lightly-armed mobile factory, prized for its ability to operate independently and construct infrastructure on distant worlds. During the past ten years its dagger-like shape was a rare sight this far away from Earth. Sev would be happy to call this a sign of revival and progress, but the beast was here only to feed on the guts of this planet, filling its belly with recycled components for whatever Apex wanted to construct elsewhere. As crazy as it sounds, everything on Mars is technically owned by some company from Earth. They were simply pulling out. The locals will not like it. Sev didn't like it.

He lowered his altitude, diving into the busy, hive-like construction complex. The sounds of machinery, squeaks of metal being crushed and hissing of pistons penetrated his cockpit. Upon reaching the spaceport, he piloted the craft down to one of the smaller landing pads in the towering shadow of the frigate. The Hesperia spaceport was a kilometer-wide square, surrounded by cranes and depots. Both of its old orbital cargo lifters were working, lifting the goods to whatever it is that Apex was building up there. All of the small cargo-haulers were also up in the air, leaving him and the huge frigate as the only landed craft. Wide tubes with connector rings were swinging from its undercarriage, some of them hooked up with small trucks, automatically leeching off their cargo.

Rolling up his rifle in that tattered flag, he created an untidy bundle. Then he stepped out on the dented, charred surface of the Hesperia spaceport and, without thinking too much, headed straight toward the wounded spider at the center of this malign web.

***

"Superintendent!"

Sev just kept walking.

"Hey! Superintendent!" The soldier wearing new hexagonal black-and-white camo uniform stepped in his way. His visor was a menacing black mirror. An upgraded rifle model rested on his chest, and an imposing armed drone rolled behind him like a pet gorilla.

The soldier was referring to a faded set of triangles on Sev's old, bleached Apex suit. Superintendent Şevket Bulut, Apex Corporation. Officially, that was his rank on some roster that wasn't updated. With a soldier barring his way, he felt the walls of the funnel effect closing in, pushing him to a place of heightened danger.

"Yes..."He struggled to remember what two straight and one broken line on the soldier's arm could signify: "...yes, foreman?"

"Only frigate crew allowed past this point. There is a drop-off station for you over there. Get lost!" He extended an armored glove at a pair of parked trucks, which were unloading cargo modules.

"Heil Hitler," Sev muttered incomprehensively and followed the instructions. Angular hull of the frigate loomed over him, like a wall. Getting inside will be hard. Supplies and components were being sucked in by pipes and drones, and he would be easy to spot walking over an empty stretch of the landing pad. Even if he could get close, there was no way in.

At the drop-off point, one of the dusty truck drivers greeted him: "Hey man. Enjoyin' the reckonin'?"

Sev knew that voice. That lazy manner of saying 'man' and chipping away every word sounded a lot like his radio pal from the MarSafari base: "Gary?"

"Ha! That's me. Have we met down in the cantina?"

"Yeah." Sev nodded naively at the balding, mustached little man. "What are you doing here?"

"Same as you, man. Packin' them up. Not much else we *can* do. They are pullin' the plug on this place. We never should've left Earth anyway. Well... at least we tried!" Gary shrugged with a stupid smile. It was a sad sight.

Something moved in the bowels of the huge frigate. A wide ramp was slowly lowered, carrying a platoon of amber-colored tanks. The impressive armored vehicles rolled over the landing pad, forming a rumbling line.

Gary shook his head: "Ha! Will ya look at that? I heard some of the locals have banded together and are still fightin' on, but then Apex rolls out the heavies and tows them all in for recyclin'. Man, it's futile."

But Sev wasn't listening to his ramblings. With everybody watching this procession of war machines, he made a dash for the scaffolding wall. Upon reaching it, he kept climbing the stairs and walking over gangways without looking back. A welding drone didn't pay attention to him as he rushed past it. He was getting tired, but he pressed on. That terrible compliance he heard in Gary's voice made him want to scream. He vented that energy into running, climbing ever higher, until he reached the top of the scaffolding, bent over and out of breath.

His jaw was shaking from it all. He didn't want to be here. This was a terrible place that made men falter, and doubt what it's all about. It all moves like a heart. Contracting, expanding and contracting again. The Dark Age, The Space Age, The Dark Age. The rhythm seemed unstoppable.

Sev stood up. Behold! The final chapter of the colonization of Mars. The Great Compression! And yet the battle for an entire planet – abandoned as it was – was waged on such a small scale. A platoon of tanks? Anokha and Iyor surely didn't have it easy up there, but a single frigate for the entire Mars sector? In times like this, a single gun *can* make a difference. With the flag bundle under his arm, Sev reached the final ladder and climbed onto the protruding wing section of the frigate.

Crouched, he made his way on to the battle-hurt hull of the ship. Small welding drones buzzed around, mending the missing armor plates. They ignored him. From up here, the broad angular body of the frigate seemed vast, the small ant-like figures mingling on the distant landing pad below, as the faraway Sun slowly died out over the Dandelion volcano to the west.

It didn't take him long to find his way in. Explosion blast from an apparent battle in orbit has dislodged several armor plates, exposing the messy understructure. This was his kind of terrain. Understructure, ruins, wreckages... Sev explored many of those whilst roaming the red planet. He dove under the steel-plated skin of the frigate, pushing away wires and kicking at charred, twisted beams to make his way deeper into the darkness. Finally he lost his ground and fell, hitting the floor of a small chamber. He was in. The room had a sloped, irregular ceiling even before the explosive makeover. Filling the niches on the walls were three modern, bone-colored EVA hardshell suits, secured and ready for use in heavy duty situations or, judging by the slash marks and bullet holes on some of them – even violent boarding actions. The fourth wall contained a standard door, obviously sealed off to contain the temporary breached hull.

Sev turned on his flashlight. This was a new breed of spacesuits, worn by some kind of battle engineers. Arms had modular hardpoints for various tools. He disconnected the grinder/welder combo tool, and connected the power cable to his own suit. Without knowing what lies on the other side, he started to cut his way through the seals on the door. As soon as he heard the air hissing and gushing from the other side he pushed the door open, closed it behind him and started to re-seal it, nervously glancing over his shoulder at the hallway he was in. It was empty.

Without thinking too much, he pressed on. He had no plan in his mind. It was far too late for that. The dimly lit octagonal hallway was lined with doors and low, wide windows on each side. In the rooms behind them soldiers without helmets ate roasted meat and laughed. After years of simpler, space-grown food Sev found their diet repulsive. He ducked out of sight and pressed on.

He tried to envision the interior of the big ship, his current position and where the hangar and helm would be. It wasn't too difficult, because modular construction always used the same building blocks in optimal, more-or-less similar alignment. On the outside, this was just a regular frigate, but in the interior he noticed unknown modules. New, complex equipment in some of the rooms, heavy duty suits; and then that improved cockpit on Raja's fighter and upgraded weapons carried by these elite soldiers. You can't just develop all this in an instant. Then it occurred to him: this entire tech existed, maybe for years, but it was kept secret, reserved only for top Apex projects like this one! For reasons unknown, real progress had been made, but it was not made public.

"It wasn't the Dark Ages everywhere. It's just that... we were kept in the dark!"

His stroll through this deceptive, high-tech frigate wouldn't be possible with the full crew onboard. But with casualties from the orbital battle and its tank company out on a mission, he had an easier time dodging Apex employees. Now he had a clear goal, and by following exposed conveyor belt tubes on the ceiling he finally reached it. The production core.

He had to pass through a small decontamination tunnel, before entering an unusually shaped control room. The noise was overwhelming! He was inside a large glass pyramid with a wide computer console at the center, overlooking various fabrication modules on the other side. Behind the triangular glass walls he could see heavy machinery rotating and extruding sheets of molten metal. Flying sparks gave the impression of a night sky filled with falling stars. And above the glass pyramid stood something magnificent. He had no idea what it was, but the symmetrical, elegant construction of the mysterious, cube-like module emanating soothing blue light filled him with wonder.

This was where the magic was happening.

The signal light above the door turned red. It was the only way in or out of this place. Someone was in the decontamination tunnel! Sev ducked behind the command console and waited.

The hissing sound of the sliding door.

Sev held his breath.

Nervous steps approaching.

Sev pushed his hand into the folds of the bundle, and felt the grip of his rifle.

A mechanical click, as if something was inserted into the console behind him.

He stood up to face whoever was on the other side.

Sunken eyes set disturbingly wide on a craggy, pale face. Graying hair. Crew cut. Very tall. Impeccable new Apex uniform. And a set of triangles, diamonds and stripes on his sleeve that spelled out his rank.

"Sand." Sev said.

Lips twisted in terror, completely taken aback at the sight of an intruder at the core of his ship, Director Sand gasped with a mix of disgust and fear: "What's going on? Are you mad!?"

"No." Sev said calmly.

"What... are you doing here? This is private property!"

"No." He lifted his bundle, long barrel protruding from the mess.

"Wait! I can call off the attack on the Ceran Frame. Is that why you're here?"

"No."

"What then? Why are you here?"

Awkwardly, they both looked down at the silver key inserted to the command console, complex blueprints rotating on each display. They looked each other in the eye again.

"No! The time is not right! Look."Director pointed up at the cube module above, but Sev kept his attention where it should be. "The Jump Drive! We applied the third law of thermodynamics. We did it thirty-two years ago! If we had just published it then, the space industry would boom uncontrollably. But we kept it a secret, and pushed here and there to force the decline, buying more and more. Now Apex owns two thirds of *everything* outside of Earth! We are on the verge of a great Unification." He brought his hand up and closed it in a fist.

"No, you're not."

"You can't steal this. You can't just... use something without having any idea how it works! It would be like giving a rifle to an ape."

Sev pulled the trigger three times in rapid succession. *Thirty two years.* Inside the gun a complicated process took place. Three times the hammer snapped forward to strike the primer. This lighted a spark, which ignited the propellant, creating an explosion that sent the bullet down the grooved barrel. *Thirty two years in an induced coma.* Part of the expanding gasses and recoil were harnessed so the extractor could remove the empty casing and make room for the next round. *Monkeys with guns.* Without him thinking about it, each time the complicated process was executed flawlessly.

Director Sand was still alive when he crashed through the glass wall and into the scrap collector below.

***

After the download was complete, Sev climbed to the service airlock and stepped out onto the vast hull of the frigate. It was a quiet night. He unrolled the shabby bundle and erected that torn

Martian flag on the main antenna.

Somewhere, a great wave smashed over red rocks, sending splashes and pebbles high into the sky. For a moment it seemed like it couldn't be stopped, but then it started to lose momentum and, slowly at first, it begun to roll back with a layer of lace-like foam on the surface as the only residue of violent impact.

***

"Thirty two years, Anokha! My entire lifetime spent in a carefully engineered decline. What a way to end the Big Expansion!" Sev's voice could be heard, as the laser signal bounced through a network of stolen satellites, connecting his MC rover and the distant Frame base.

"But it *is* over." she replied with a tired grin. "We seem to have gotten the worst part of it. The very end."

"What comes next?"

Anokha sighed: "Well, Ceran refugees are in shambles, but at least we have Apex on the run. You should have seen the battle, Sev. It was their moment of brilliance! Iyor faked retreat before the battlecruiser, goading it into an ambush. They fought so intensely and severely damaged it. But... it simply distorted and vanished before we could board it! The whole ship – pooh! And the fabricator frigate has departed Mars, too. I expected to hear from that gloating Director Sand, but even he fell silent. Now we will never get a hold of that jump drive technology."

"I have it all." Sev announced unceremoniously.

"You have what?"

"The jump drive blueprint, cryogenic module, improved atmospheric thrusters, gravity generators, new structural grids..."

There was a hollow pause on the other side, but then she came back, her voice carefully excited: "You little weasel! You stole it from them, didn't you? When you send those over here we'll be able to match everything they have!"

"No. Everybody gets this tech. Not only the Cerans."

"Everybody? But think about it. That would also mean Pirates, and... Are you sure about this?"

"No, I'm not. But I've already done it. Everything has been uploaded to a public satellite. It's broadcasting the data. Any minute now the signal will reach Apex HQ back on Earth, and they will know that everybody knows. Everyone will have direct access to a product of thirty years of compression. Progress really does beat on like a heart."

"You know Sev, you have a knack for productive betrayal." She paused. "But, if you give access to something so powerful to everyone..."

"This tech is not magic. Well, not anymore. It's still a complex piece of machinery that requires rare metals to construct, high engineering skills to assemble and immense amount of power to operate, limiting its use."

"So that's why they were building that colossal solar collector above Mars! But still... arming everyone with this invention would mean nobody is safe from sudden attacks."

"Anokha, this changes everything. A new, unnamed age is upon us." His voice had never sounded so certain. "The... topography of Space has changed. Inside the Solar System, everybody having this tech is like nobody is having it, since no one has the upper hand. And why squabble over these few planets, when we can reach further now? If we can somehow build a vessel with enough power, we could reach distant stars in only a few long jumps."

"You know, it's funny that you say that. These refugees are itching for a new place to settle. If we can somehow combine the unfinished solar collector with The Frame, we will have a powerhouse. And..." she made an intentional pause. "Lero from Vladivostok has sent me a message just an hour ago. He has pinpointed where the mysterious signal that disrupted the Narwhal emanated from. He is on his way here."

"Well, that sounds like an expedition is forming up. Will you be able to join us, Anokha?"

"Perhaps. But you will have to wait for me, as I have other plans first." She was silent for a while, but it was the silence of somebody smiling on the other side. "I'm going home."

7. The Hymn of refuges

My name is Iyor. I discover myself again, for the hundredth time. And for the hundredth time, I am amazed. I feel like I am getting older and beginning to know things. But with knowledge comes *fear.* It has been building up my whole life, and I mistook it for a herald of wisdom. Now I see things as they truly are: an endless abyss surrounds our Frame, invisible currents pulling us in all directions. This emptiness has always been there, but we tend to focus on the bright dots, not the soul-diluting void in between. Space is a bad place to turn wise.

Preparing for our journey, we sing an eerie hymn in a multitude of languages. Nobody expects us to endure, but we cannot quit either. One generation off-planet and our ligaments are already forgetting gravity. And, freed from it, we are flying higher. Or are we diving deeper? I am not sure anymore. True freedom is a terrifying concept.

But the perpetual victory in conquering of Space was interrupted in recent years. The pervasive feeling of shrinking horizons bleached all hope. We found our destiny shattered by doubt. Maybe we are not fated to be a space-faring race after all? Gods have abandoned us, and in doing so, were abandoned themselves. Now, when we look into the heavens we don't see a limitless, ever-expanding ocean of possibilities. We see only the void – and we have nothing to fear.

THE END

Afterword

The novel was written in three months listening to Chroma Key, Shlohmo, Nick Cave and Fleet Foxes. It's the first proper-sized novel I've written. It took me some time to deal with the publishing process, and in the meantime I've written another one, a fast paced cyberpunk story titled *Four Zero Four*. Writing is not too hard. You should try it.

Why did I have to tell this story?

When talking with the astronauts that have been up there they will always tell you things like: "Earth looks magnificent from orbit, all shiny and blue." I especially like the guy who landed on the Moon to take the famous picture of... Earth. Are you kidding me? Why spend the effort to leave if you are going to look back? The simple truth is that there is nothing else to see, we are afraid of the big, empty, dark places and we keep looking back at Mother for support. When we are down here, safe in her embrace we dare look at the stars and dream of being astronauts, but when we are up there we don't stare at the void for too long. There is nothing to see. The distances are simply too big. We can't breathe. The radiation kills us. That's hard science, no messing around.

And so we add a bit of fiction to science to comfort us.

Appendix

Good computer games are easily recognizable - they have no beginning and no end. They take a step back and merely provide *tools of entertainment,* to be constantly interpreted and reinvented by the community. I've played a sandbox game called Space Engineers for years, contributing with my creations in this growing universe. Now I went so far as to write an SF novel based on it.

Janitors of the Late Space Age is by no means the official storyline of the game. It is not sponsored, but it is acknowledged by Keen Software House, the creators of the game. It has no relation to the game and it also has no relationship to the character or the story of the game. It was merely inspired by it. It features the same technology level, modular spaceship design, vast, empty reaches of space and desolate planets providing endless possibilities. All this, spiced up with that characteristic, unfathomable mishaps and accidents that sometimes happen.

The story is a product of an open and active community, something Space Engineers always excelled in and I am happy that game's creators gave me the green light to go on and present this novel to you, the reader.

Made in the USA
San Bernardino, CA
15 November 2018